W9-BNF-965

The Ivory Lyre

Also by Shirley Rousseau Murphy

Nightpool

Shirley Rousseau Murphy

The Ivory Lyre

1 8 1 7

HARPER & ROW, PUBLISHERS

Cambridge, Philadelphia, San Francisco, Washington, London, Mexico City, São Paolo, Singapore, Sydney

NEW YORK

Designed by Joyce Hopkins
2 3 4 5 6 7 8 9 10

Library of Congress Cataloging-in-Publication Data
Murphy, Shirley Rousseau.
    The ivory lyre.

    Summary: With the help of four shape-shifting dragons,
dragonbards Tebriel and Kiri are instrumental in inciting
an uprising against the dark and in locating the magical
ivory lyre.
    [1. Fantasy] I. Title
PZ7.M956Iv 1987   [Fic]   85-45831
ISBN 0-06-024362-7
ISBN 0-06-024363-5 (lib. bdg.)

For Antonia Markiet

CHAPTER

1

The four dragons fled through the sky, their wings hiding stars, the wind of their passing churning the sea below. The two black dragons were nearly hidden against the night, but the two white ones shone bright as sweeping clouds. The larger white dragon carried a rider, a slim lad. He was barely sixteen, well muscled, tanned, dressed in stolen leathers, with a stolen sword at his side. He stared down between the white dragon's beating wings at occasional islands fast overtaken. Then he looked ahead with rising anger at the island that was this night's target. His rage matched the dragons' fury for what they sensed there on Birrig.

"The dark unliving rule there," the dragons screamed. "They are soul killers—the dark side of mortal. . . ."

"Yes," Tebriel answered, "but they will die. We free Birrig this night."

They dove in a rush of wind, Teb bent low to see between Seastrider's wings as the dragons dropped toward Birrig's wood.

Meadows lay on the far side of the island, dotted by eight villages. The dragons gained the shore on widespread wings, then folded their wings close to their sides and slipped in among the twisted oaks of the grove in silence, pressing under the great branches, the leaves sliding noiselessly across their scales. Teb slid down.

He paced the wood, then returned to stand beside Seastrider, listening with his mind and inner senses just as the four dragons did. They could see in their minds the dark leaders who ruled here, and knew that the enslaved islanders slept a sleep as featureless as death. Even waking they would know little pain or wonder, so drugged were they with the powers of the dark. The dragons moved deeper among the giant trees. To be discovered was too great a danger, not for themselves, but for the cause they served.

"There are nine leaders," Teb said softly, stroking Seastrider's white cheek. She leaned her head against him, feeling his hatred of the dark; their thoughts were in perfect sympathy, these two who were so powerfully paired.

They are sheltered in the stone manor house, she said in silence. *Two of the true dark, the unliving, and seven humans turned to the ways of the dark.* She scraped her scales nervously against the rough sides of the oaks.

The other three dragons moved uneasily. Teb walked among them, touching and reassuring them. He could feel their tension nearly exploding, their hatred of the

2

dark grown to a force almost visible in its intensity. It matched his own.

Of the dark leaders they saw in vision, five slept. Two of the humans were awake, locked in obscene embrace with the two unliving. The unliving never slept, though they never seemed to come fully to life, either. The pale, man-shaped beings were as coldly expressionless as spiders. Their color would rise a little at the lure of new evil or lust. They sucked upon men's spirits and souls as certain spiders suck upon human blood.

Teb stood a moment filled with disgust, putting down his instinctive fear. *Un-men, unliving, you will not take this land, not while dragons live to defeat you. You will give back the minds you have robbed. We will take* them back.

In the vision that Teb and the dragons shared, the blank faces of the sleeping villagers were scarred and bruised and dirty. Many slept on the ground, tied by ropes to their places of work, too obedient to the dark to untie themselves. The miller was shackled beside the mill wheel; a carpenter sprawled among logs and tools; shepherds were leg-tied together beside a dung heap. A small child with a twisted arm lay huddled on rags in the corner of a barn, tied to a post where she had been pounding grain.

The dragons were clawing now into the soft mulch of the forest, tense with rage at the slavery the dark had created, ready to battle it. Teb leaped to Sea-strider's back, stroked her. *Now*, he said, *now begin,* and power filled them as they raised their voices in song, dragon and boy.

Power swelled as they made visions explode in the minds of the sleeping slaves. *Now you will see truly once more.* They warped time into another dimension so that the past came alive. People long dead came alive, as real as Teb himself. A forgotten time exploded into life, a time before Birrig was slave to the dark.

Now, suddenly, busy people filled the lanes and sheepfolds, shearing, lambing, making the dyes and grooming the wool and weaving the fine tapestries for which Birrig was famous. Loud, hard-living people. Dragon song brought alive the hot glances of the young as they sought their mates. A girl cuddled a baby. Small children ran among the looms. The blending voices of bard and dragon peopled the village and filled the minds of the present-day slaves, who woke and stumbled to their doors to gape. Before them in the streets, the past lived.

Folk came forth hesitantly, out into the busy lanes. They stepped into a world nothing like their drab one, and their faces lost confusion and brightened with understanding.

Untie yourselves, Teb shouted in song, *tear off your chains.*

Men and women fought to free themselves and reached out to touch the strangers who were their own ancestors. They could not touch them, yet were not perplexed.

The past is the lost part of you, Teb shouted. *Feel*

4

whole again, now; defeat the dark, now. . . .

The child inside the barn was awake, tearing at the knots of her ropes. Freed, she stood for a moment not knowing what to do. Then she began to run. She ran in circles around the cottages, in and out among her ancestors like a colt gone wild.

Folk began to approach the woods, coming to the call of the songs. They moved through the Birrig of the present and the Birrig of the past all at once, seeking the source of the magic. But not all came toward the woods; some approached the manor house. The nine dark leaders stood there in the doorway shoulder to shoulder, their evil like a dark stench seeping around the building.

Destroy them, Teb said in song. *It is your privilege to destroy them.*

"The dark leaders know we are here," Seastrider said to him.

"They must not carry the news beyond this island," said Nightraider. "They must not live to do so."

"They will not live," said Tebriel. "Look." He stretched up to see over the topmost branches, but he need not have. They could see it in their minds, the townsfolk drawing closer to the dark leaders, who backed away.

Now, Teb shouted. *Now . . . It is your choice to kill them. They are the slave masters, they have murdered your children, they steal the world from you when they take your memory.* . . .

The people of Birrig began to move toward the dark

5

leaders, slowly and with purpose. The faces of the unliving turned from gray-tinged to deathly pale, and they mouthed enchantments. The faces of the seven humans who had willingly embraced the dark twisted into masks of terror, but Teb felt no regret for them. They had chosen this evil freely. If it had not been for their kind, the unliving would never have conquered these lands. An un-man screamed a curse, two humans turned to flee; and then the town was on them.

Teb slid down from Seastrider's back. The other three dragons pressed close, to nuzzle him. He hated the killing, but it had to be done. The townsfolk truly had a right. And the dark must not be allowed to leave Birrig to spread word that there were singing dragons on Tirror. Not yet. Secrecy was their weapon. They were too few in number now; they must find other bards. He hoped they would find other dragons. They were not an army yet, and it would take an army of bards and dragons to free all of Tirror. The freedom fighters, secretly at work in many lands, could free men's bodies but could not free their spirits; only the dragonbards could. If the dark thought it had driven out all the dragons and bards, if it thought Teb himself was dead, then let it believe that. It gave Teb more time. He watched the awakened slaves destroy their dark masters; then he and the dragons rose into the dawn sky, climbing fast to hide themselves among clouds. They made their way south to the Lair and the dragon nest.

The wind of their wings tore a storm across the sky

that lashed at the branches of their nest as they descended. They circled the high, bare mountain peak once, then landed within the nest's walls. It was like a fort made of great trees pulled up by the roots. The dragons preened themselves, cleaning their wings, wanting a short nap as is the way with dragons. Seastrider yawned, her mouth like a closet bristling with rows of white swords. She curled down beside her brothers and sister, their wings folded, their heads resting on tangles of smaller branches. Teb climbed the logs that formed the lip of the nest.

The wind hit him so fiercely it would have swept him over if he hadn't held on to a thrusting branch. His dark hair whipped around his face, tugging loose from the leather band that tied it. He stood looking down at the land more than a mile below.

His view of Tirror and the southern islands was much as he would see in flight. Directly below him was the Bay of Dubla; beyond it, the small continent of Windthorst; then the sea stained red with the rising sun. He could see the Palace of Auric, a pale dot in the south of Windthorst. It was his palace, his kingdom, stolen from his family when his father was murdered. Teb had been held captive there as a child by his father's killers. His father's loyal horsemaster, together with the speaking animals, had helped him escape from those dark leaders when he was twelve.

His sister, Camery, had been left behind in the tower. But now she, too, was free, somewhere on Tirror, thanks again to Garit, the horsemaster.

East of Auric, beyond Windthorst's coast, lay a tiny island. He knew every detail of Nightpool—the black rock caves, the green inner meadow and hidden lake. He had lived there for four years among the otter nation after he had escaped his captors. He missed the furry, fish-smelling otters. They had shaken water over him and nattered at him and chased him in the sea. They had cared for him all during his long illness when he hadn't known who he was. He wondered, when he stood thinking of them like this, if the white leader, Thakkur, might be standing in the sacred meeting cave seeing a vision of him in the magical clamshell. He missed the island with its cozy caves, the gatherings and feasts. He missed Nightpool.

He wasn't homesick for the palace at Auric. Rather, it was a surge of fury he felt, of hatred for the men who had destroyed his family. He knew a cold desire to take back his own, to avenge his father's death, to avenge the mistreatment of Camery. He would bet any amount that she and Garit had gotten themselves involved in one underground army or another. He meant to find out which. He meant to find her, find both of them. He had perhaps already had a hint of her, but he wasn't sure.

Three days ago, he and the four dragons had ridden a westerly wind over the land of Edain, and Nightraider had sensed the presence of a bard, a woman, and had descended fast to the unpeopled shore to search. They had found no one, but Teb had sensed a fleeting vision of golden hair, the clean line of a young woman's jaw, and was certain it was Camery.

"There was a bard here on this place," Nightraider had said, his great yellow eyes blazing with fierce loss as he reared up to search the cliff above the cave. The black dragon had lingered on the empty shore long after Teb and the other three had left. When he returned he was downcast. Teb knew Nightraider had found a hint of his bard in Edain, but no more than a hint. No clue that would lead him to her.

"The dark has hidden her," the black dragon had bellowed, spitting flame.

"Perhaps," Teb said. "Or maybe she hid herself. If it *was* Camery. Maybe she doesn't know what she is. No one ever told me that I was of dragonbard blood."

He had not realized his own destiny until years after the dark leader Sivich had tried to use him as bait to trap a singing dragon. He'd had no idea his mother was a dragonbard, and he was sure Camery hadn't, either. Their mother had left them, riding away from the palace leading a pack horse. She had not returned. Their father would not explain. Later she had been reported drowned. It was not until years later, when Teb found her diary, that he knew she was still alive and learned she was a dragonbard, gone to seek her own dragon.

Seastrider began to dream, shivering, then shook herself awake. She stared at Teb with huge green eyes, then reached out to touch him with one lethal ivory claw as long as his forearm.

"We will hunt, Tebriel. Let us hunt."

She spread her wings suddenly, rearing above the nest and staring seaward, then dropped down so Teb could mount. Knowing what was coming, he pulled off his sheepskin coat and boots, mounted, and tucked his cold feet against her warm sides. She soared west on a veering, icy wind out over the open sea. Teb clung and held his breath as she dove. The icy water closed over them, nearly knocking him off, his fists gripped hard in the white leather harness, his knees and feet tucked under it. The ice cold shocked him but turned to tingling warmth as his blood surged, the pressure of the water hard against him. The green water sped around him filled with light as Seastrider pursued the fish ahead. Teb let out his breath a little at a time, as the otters had taught him. Soon Seastrider was up, breaking surface, with a red shark twice the length of a man clutched squirming in her teeth.

"Not shark again," Teb shouted. "I'm tired of shark. Can't you catch a salmon?"

There are no salmon this time of year, she said in silence. She bit the shark deep enough to kill it and turned back for the Lair, where Teb stripped out of his pants and tunic. He hung them to dry beside his small fire while he cooked his shark steak. The other dragons hunted, the smaller female to the south, her white body flashing against the sea, the two black males ranging out westward until they were lost from view in the gray sky. Seastrider left him twice for more shark, for the dragons liked large breakfasts.

She also brought him a small golden sea trout and dropped it at his feet as the other dragons settled in, dripping quantities of water over the nest.

The trout caused an argument among them. Starpounder said Seastrider was spoiling Teb. They began to tussle, rocking the nest so hard Teb thought they would push it off the mountain peak, thrashing up into the sky, stirring a wind like a hurricane.

They descended at last, grinning at one another as only dragons can grin, and settled down side by side on the nest. It was still early, the sun barely up.

They could not do their work in daylight. Seastrider sighed and curled down in a tight coil against the side of the nest with the others. Teb stood watching them, feeling depressed in spite of the morning's work.

They were too few. The other three dragons had no human bards to complete their magic. He didn't even know whether there were any more bards on Tirror besides Camery, *if* she really had inherited their mother's talent. He could remember her singing, innocently following their mother's voice when they were small. Neither of them had guessed, then, what their song could mean someday. He meant to find her, and the best way was to join the underground. He didn't feel ready, but the time was close. He didn't like to think he was afraid.

CHAPTER

2

Teb watched the dragons stir and wake. All four turned to look at him. Even to a dragonbard, those four stares all at once, bright and intent, were unnerving. He frowned, trying to understand what they were thinking.

He had an impression of journey, of wheeling flight. But they did that every morning. He had an impression of cobbled streets and dim city doorways seen close at hand, of palaces and crowds of people and the smell of taverns. Yes, their sleeping thoughts had been the same as his waking ones. It is time, Teb thought. Time for me to go into the cities.

The dragons nodded.

He felt shrunken and small knowing he would walk alone and earthbound when for so long he had soared aloft between the wings of dragons and had been protected by dragons.

But he and the dragons had done their work on nearly all the smaller continents. Only a few islands were left. Their usefulness through song was nearly gone for the present. The larger lands were ruled by the dark, except for half a dozen, and one bard and four dragons could not free the minds of a whole continent at one time. The dragons would be discovered, the dark put on alert. They must play the game close until their band was larger.

He must join the underground. He must search for bards. He must learn the ways of the resistance, and how best to help it. He must make himself and the dragons known to the resistance, so they could plan together for the greater battles to come.

"Yes," said Seastrider. "Yes. But you will not go alone."

He stared at her. What nonsense was this? He had always known that when the time came, he must go into the cities alone. "What do you plan to do?" he asked her, touching her great silver cheek. "Walk the roads pretending to be my war-horse?"

"Yes," she said. "I will do that."

Teb wished she could. It wasn't a moment for joking.

"I will shape-shift. We have spoken of it before. It is not impossible."

"But you said it was unreliable, with the powers of the dark so strong. Even if you could make shape-shifting magic strong enough to counter the dark, it could be dangerous. You said you might not be able to change back."

"With practice, Tebriel, we will manage. Nothing in this life is without danger."

"And what do you mean by *we*?"

"One saddle horse and three to follow you." Seastrider stretched out over the lip of the nest, her wings spread on the wind so she hung motionless in the sky. Then she turned and curled down into a tight circle. Suddenly she vanished.

In her place reared a dazzling white mare, her neck bowed and her green eyes blazing. Teb stood gaping.

Then Starpounder disappeared, and where the blue-black dragon had coiled there wheeled a snorting blue-black stallion. Then Nightraider, two stallions and a mare now, and then Windcaller. So two and two they were, their eyes flashing with powerful magic.

"How can you do that?" Teb said, caught in wonder. "How can your bodies compress so? How . . . ?"

We do not compress, Seastrider managed to tell him. *Our bodies are caught in another dimension. What you see of us is the stuff of magic, of the shape-shifting spell, and not real.*

Teb touched her shoulder and neck, and wove his fingers in her mane. She felt very real to him, warm and silken, with the wild, sweet smell of a good horse. He put his hand on her back. She stayed steady. He tightened his hand in her mane and with a sudden thrust leaped across her back and swung astride. She stood quivering and snorting; then she reared and pawed in a battle stance, so he had to grip tight with his knees. She galloped in a small circle, leaping logs, then stood quiet, sweating.

Will I do? she asked demurely.

"Oh, yes. Only . . . you are too beautiful. All of you are. You will attract too much attention."

Seastrider lowered her head and looked at him with wry teasing that made him laugh. *We cannot help being beautiful, Tebriel. Dragons are the most beautiful creatures alive, and so we have become beautiful horses.* They had no false modesty, these dragons.

Teb sighed. "Not only will you make me more conspicuous," he said, "but the armies of the dark would like very much to have such mounts as you. What will you do if they try to steal you?"

When she did not answer, he grew annoyed. He knew her silences. "What kind of plan are you cooking? Do you *want* to be stolen? But what good—"

Not stolen, Tebriel. You will travel as a horse trader, and we will be your wares. Such fine mounts as we should give you entrée into any palace on Tirror.

"And may I ask where I have secured such horses? And what you mean to do if someone buys you? What—"

Seastrider's look silenced him. *You will call yourself a prince from the far southern land of Thedria, which lies beyond the vast expanse of sea and has no commerce with these lands. The dark knows little of that place, I think, for we have sensed no evil from that far continent. You will steal appropriate clothes for a prince, and you will enter the strongholds of the dark in style. And,* she said, tossing her head, *if we are bought, Tebriel, no matter. No stable or fence or stone prison can hold us.*

"Well," he said. "Well . . . all right. But how have I come to these continents? By rowboat over the wild seas hauling four horses?"

By seagoing barge, to barter your horses for gold. You are the Prince of the Horsemasters of Thedria.

She had it all worked out. Teb pointed out to her civilly that he had not intended to go among palaces but to slip quietly into the cities among the common folk, where he could gather information unnoticed by the dark rulers. If it was all the same to Seastrider, he did not want to make himself an object of immediate observation for the dark.

But if you are an object of great interest to the dark, Tebriel, do you not think the underground will be watching you even more closely? Do you not think they will be more than anxious to learn about you, and to learn which side you might favor, this very rich and mysterious prince? It will be much easier to let the underground soldiers come to you, Tebriel, than to try to search them out in strange cities.

Teb sighed again and said no more. The horses disappeared and the dragons were there, still staring in that annoying way. He stared back at them crossly, then turned away to ready his pack.

He wrapped his mother's diary in oilskins, with a few other valuables he would not take, and hid them between tree trunks in the wall of the nest. He would take the large packet that contained the white leather from which he had cut Seastrider's harness, and the awl he had used to fashion it. He would need more

16

thread. He slipped the gold coins into his pocket, gifts from the otter nation. With gold he could steal clothes, yet leave payment.

He knew where they would go—they had discussed it several times: Dacia, which lay far to the north above a tangle of island nations. Neutral Dacia. They had swung low on the night wind near to it more than once, and always they could sense the powers of the dark there. Yet the dark did not rule Dacia. He didn't understand how this could be, how that country had remained neutral. Both dark and resistance forces were strong on Dacia. He didn't know what had kept the dark from possessing that country totally, for the small continent provided good cover for the dark forces. From that base, the unliving could attack Edain and Bukla and the tiny island nations of the Benaynne Archipelago.

Surely the resistance had a strong spy network and ways to steal food and weapons from the dark armies. Perhaps the strength of the resistance alone was what kept Dacia free, though Teb felt there might be a stronger force at work. He would be very interested to learn why Dacia was not beaten back by the dark, yet had not driven it out. Dacia would be a likely place to find Garit, and maybe Camery, a good place to join the rebels in any case.

The truly free countries were very aggressive in destroying the unliving, for most humans felt only terror of the wraithlike creatures. The very mention of the leader Quazelzeg made warriors burn with hatred.

The slave makers sucked on the suffering of humans as a leech will suck human blood. Fear in humans strengthened the un-men, and pain in humans and animals was as heady as wine to them. They would devise any means to increase and lengthen such suffering.

But if Ebis the Black had driven them out, and had kept his land free, so could others. Teb and the dragons had gone twice to Ratnisbon, to sing the past alive for Ebis's people. Ebis understood that people needed that knowledge of Tirror's past, of their own pasts; otherwise they had no memory, no knowledge of themselves, and no notion of who they really were or what choices they had in life. Ebis's people wanted to make their own choices and would not allow the dark to rob them of that freedom.

The dragon song kept freedom alive in people's minds, stirring their fury against the smothering and consuming dark. That was what it must do for all of Tirror. There *were* more bards; there had to be. Perhaps, somewhere, there were more dragons. The old power, where bard could speak to bard or dragon over distances, was all muddled and frayed by the dark. Teb caught only glimpses of battles. He knew there was little communication remaining among the resistance forces, human or animal. This, too, Teb and the dragons meant to change. Meanwhile, they would be in the thick of it in Dacia, and would learn more.

They waited until dark before taking to the sky, moving on the silent wind over the small island nations. It was near to midnight when Teb chose a likely-looking fishing town from which to steal his new clothes.

They came down along the cave-ridden cliffs of Bukla and, because black Nightraider would not be seen so easily, it was he who turned himself into a horse and carried Teb up the cliffs to the prosperous little town.

Teb jimmied a shop door with little trouble. He chose his clothes with care by the shielded light of one lantern taken from the shop desk. He selected three changes of the most elegant tunics and dark leggings, a pair of fine boots, and a red cape that stirred memories, for its color. These were clothes meant to impress, suited to a rich prince, not to his personal preference. He found buckles, heavy linen thread, and some felted horsehair padding for a saddle in the shop's workroom, and packed it all into a linen bag. He left ample gold in exchange, and locked the door behind him.

They spent three days on a small rock island while Teb fashioned the four halters, a saddle, and saddlebags of the white leather. Then on the fourth night the dragons made for the northerly and deserted shore of Dacia, north of the city, some five miles from the black palace that loomed against the stars.

CHAPTER
3

The Palace of Dacia was built directly into the mountain, so its deepest chambers were the mountain's own stony caves. The sheer black palace walls, carved and ornate, looked down on the country's one city, their arrow slits watching the teeming streets like thin, appraising eyes. The city climbed up so abruptly to meet the palace that the stone huts stood jumbled nearly on top of one another, straw-thatched roofs shouldering against the doorsteps above.

It was early evening now, the sun gone behind the mountain. The palace's heavy shadow spread down across the tangled city, reaching to swallow more and more houses and lanes as suppertime drew near. The smell of the city was of boiled mutton and cabbage and of animal dung and crowded humanity. Men were coming home from the wharves and fields and pouring out of taverns. Women shuffled pots on cookstoves and shouted at squalling babies.

Kiri stood in her own darkened doorway, listening.

She glanced back inside once, where her grandmother dozed on the cot, her thin body angled under the frayed quilt, her veined hands clasped together.

Kiri watched Gram with tenderness, then turned to make her way up the darker side of the cobbled street, deeper into the shadow of the palace. She was fourteen, thin, sun-browned, her brown hair tucked up under a green cap. She was dressed in the green homespun tunic of a page. She wore a sharpened kitchen knife hidden beneath the tunic, couched comfortably against her thigh. As she climbed, the city spread itself out below her. She could see the first early squares of candlelight, and the occasional brighter glow of an oil lamp in some privileged household—Kiri took note of which houses. There, the baker was burning oil, where he had not in nearly a month. What had he been up to, to curry favor with the king? And the tanner, also— two bright lamps in his windows.

There was a look about Kiri that was difficult to define, though she tried her best to look unremarkable. Her two tunics were purposely worn and shabby, her hair dulled by rubbing dust into her comb, her expression spiritless and unrevealing. But beneath the seeming dullness was a spark as free and wild as a mountain deer, hidden as best she could hide it. The clean chiseling of her face and the challenging, longing look in her dark eyes did not belong to the kind of drudge she pretended to be. It was a joy at night to strip out of her confining cap and brush her hair clean and talk with Gram in the privacy of their cottage, to hear

Gram's tales before the cookfire, and laugh, and not have to look so solemn and stupid.

Gram's tales were sometimes about Kiri's father, who once had been horsemaster to the king. It was a prestigious position. The horsemaster of any kingdom on Tirror was a most important person and responsible in good part for the strength of that country's armies. Now Kiri's father had gone away. He was not Gram's son; Gram was Kiri's mother's mother. But Gram respected him. Neither Gram nor Kiri spoke about the thing that had been done to him. Kiri missed him. She did not miss her mother, who had been dead since Kiri was two. She had died of the plague that Kiri and her father had escaped, though everyone around them had been sick. Kiri didn't know why this was except maybe it was because of the special talent that she and her father shared. It made her sad to think that because Mama had not shared this gift she had died. It was after Mama died that Gram came to live with them and look after Kiri.

The Queen of Dacia had also had the plague, though she didn't die of it. She was made crippled and weak, and so ill the king shut her away in a private chamber. She might as well have been dead, for all most folk spoke or cared about her; certainly not the king. He had bedded with Kiri's cousin Accacia until some mysterious event put a stop to that.

Now as she climbed the narrow cobbled street, Kiri kept her eyes cast down, watching the city under her lashes. Suddenly she heard horses and commotion. She raced to where she could see the main approach to the palace gates. She saw a slim man on a white mount. He was elegantly dressed in a red cape and gold tunic.

He rode with easy grace the shying, sidestepping war-horse. Three other horses followed him, mincing, tossing their heads, but held lightly on thin leads. He appeared far too regal and too wealthy to be traveling this land alone, and with four of the most wonderful horses Kiri had ever imagined, horses that surely had not come from Dacia or any of the surrounding countries.

They were taller than Dacian horses, for one thing, and slimmer of leg. They carried themselves with a balance and grace that no Dacian horse could match. Their necks and shoulders were dark with sweat and their legs spattered with mud from the road as if they had had a long journey. But still they were dancing and bowing their necks, their tails switching with high spirits and challenge.

When Kiri reached the small palace gate that led to the servants' quarters, she paused to watch the rider enter the main gate ahead. First she heard the creak of the gatekeeper's small door, then words exchanged that she could not make out. She could see figures stirring inside the courtyard. The great gates clanged open and the horses' hooves rang on the cobbles. When rider and horses had disappeared inside, there was more conversation muffled by the wall. Kiri waited until the gate had been closed and the gatekeeper gone back into his cottage; then she climbed the palace wall in deep shadow, her bare feet knowing the toeholds.

She slipped over the top between the iron spikes like a sparrow hopping between spears, scraping her arm only once as she eased down the other side. Who was this elegant rider, to come alone to Sardira's palace with such horses? The voices inside the courtyard had challenged him, and then had gone soft and smooth as syrup. What was his business? No one traveled on any business these days that did not have to do with the wars.

Kiri moved silently through a narrow passage to the back door of the servants' quarters, then inside. Half a dozen women looked up dully from where they were scrubbing clothes. They never remarked on her comings and goings or even noticed them, so muddled had their minds become with the nightly rations of drugged liquor. She went quickly through the dim room to the inner hall that led to the courtyard, and along this toward the tangle of voices, pressing close to the damp stone walls. She could hear the traveler giving directions for stabling his horses. He sounded young. She stood in deep shadow where she could see out into the cobbled yard.

He *was* young, not much older than she, a slim, tanned boy with high cheekbones and dark hair tied back neatly, and dark eyes. And what strange directions he was giving. A triple ration of oats—well, that was all right. But no rubdown or grooming? And the stall doors to be left wide open, the horses unfettered so they could roam at will?

"But there are no fences," the king's steward said. "Surely you don't mean . . . ?"

"They will not leave," the young man said, with an impatient scowl at the steward.

"I can't be responsible for such a thing." The steward stood stolidly, his square face sour with this challenge to his good sense. No one left horses to roam free and expected them not to stray.

"The horses are not to be tethered or confined. They will not tolerate confinement. They will be here when I want them."

The horses did seem nervous within the confinement of the courtyard. They moved and shifted close around the young man and kept glancing up past the top of the high stone wall toward the freedom beyond, as if it would not take much for them to leap that eight-foot stone barrier and be gone. Kiri had no doubt they could leap it, these tall, finely muscled creatures. She thought the slim white halters they wore would hardly hold them if they were to rear or pull back. And the saddle mare wore no bit in her mouth.

This lad was a very skilled horseman if he had trained these mounts himself. She could see that they loved him, that they remained steady only because he was there with them. What would they do in the stable, with strange grooms? Kiri stood watching the beautiful animals hungrily, just as Papa would have done. Oh, Papa would covet these horses. Papa . . . she bit her lip and pushed thoughts of Papa to the back of her mind, and studied the rider more carefully.

A white leather thong, like the leather of the halters, tied back his smooth dark hair. His face looked strong and, Kiri thought, honest. His red cape was of soft, fine wool. His tunic was gold with red trim over dark-brown leggings. His boots were made by a master craftsman.

He removed the saddlebags and the mare's saddle deftly—such a thin saddle, little more than a white leather pad—and caressed her neck and ears as if he were loath to send her with the grooms who had come into the courtyard. As they led the horses away, the mare looked back at the lad.

When they passed Kiri, all four horses twitched their ears in her direction. The nearer stallion gazed directly at her, directly into her eyes. His look froze her so that she stood dumb, staring as they passed on out of the yard.

She stood still long after the horses had gone and the young man had left the courtyard accompanied by the king's marshal, in the direction of the great hall. Her mind, her whole being, seemed frozen with the stallion's deep, searching look.

She roused herself at last and fled for the hall, to listen. Who was this man? And why did the intent stare of his horses set her blood to pounding? Her wrists prickled with the thought of magic, but she put that down to excitement. She must be levelheaded, clear-minded if she was to gather information accurately.

Her way was dark and close, between storage chambers and through back passages, until she reached the big indoor cistern that stood behind the fireplace of the great hall. This cistern heated the water for the kitchens, and its iron sides were warm against her as she slid around it, to stand between cistern and stone wall, pressed tight in the small space.

She put her ear to the wall where, with her help, mortar had long since crumbled away from between two stones. She could hear the voices in the hall clearly. The stranger was there, and the king himself, and the king's son, Abisha.

Kiri peered through and could see Abisha's plump, silk-clad legs stretched before the hearth. King Sardira, in black robes that seemed an extension of his black beard and locks, looked very pale and lined. Too much feasting, Gram would have said. Too much wine on the table. Or too much of the white powder they gave to the slaves and sometimes indulged in themselves, Kiri thought.

She could see the stranger, too. Was that a touch of humor in his dark eyes, in the lines around his mouth? One did not usually smile in the presence of King Sardira, and this stranger seemed to be holding back a laugh. Kiri liked his looks—but she knew better than to rely on a first glimpse. She pressed her ear to the hole, and listened.

CHAPTER
4

The voice of the king came clearly through the little hole in the mortar. The stone was cool and smooth against Kiri's cheek. She could hear the ring of china as Prince Abisha poured out mithnon liquor and tea. She saw the stranger shake his head.

"No mithnon, please. Just tea."

"You came from Thorley how long ago, Prince Tebmund?" The king had a way of speaking that always insinuated he did not believe one. So, the stranger was a prince.

"Several weeks," Prince Tebmund said casually. "I had some errands in the more southerly continents."

Kiri peered through the mortar hole to study him. She knew nothing about Thorley except that it was a small principality in the east of Thedria, which lay far to the south across hostile seas. Folk in this hemisphere knew little about its people. Kiri had heard they were peaceful and reputed to raise fine horses. She leaned against the stone, listening intently as Prince

Tebmund and the king discussed the sale of the four horses. Oh, how could he bear to sell such horses?

"I can promise up to fifty head of trained war-horses like these, if Your Highness desires," Prince Tebmund said. He had a quiet, clipped voice that Kiri found appealing. As if he did not care for long speeches.

King Sardira leaned back in the settee, stroked his black beard, and belched delicately. He was like a thin black bat with its wings folded neatly across its front and its black eyes missing nothing. "And what is your price, per head? I expect it will be higher for the stallions."

"It is the same for both. Two hundred pieces of gold." Prince Tebmund's expression was calm, but his dark eyes held a flash of impatience—or dislike for the king.

There was a cold pause before the king spoke. Prince Abisha remained silent. Kiri could see his fat foot tapping softly.

"Two hundred for these four," the king said. "That seems rather steep. But, of course, if they—"

"Two hundred per head," said Prince Tebmund. His dark eyes and lean face hid a surge of anger, subtle as the passing of a breath.

This pause was colder, and lengthy. Prince Abisha came to stand before the hearth, his fat stomach not inches from Kiri. She drew back against the cistern.

"It is too much," said Abisha. "It is out of the question. No one asks such gold for horses."

"These are not common horses," said Prince Tebmund.

"They are the finest horses on Tirror, as I'm sure you can see for yourselves. They will carry a man into battle with absolute absence of fear. They will not only carry him, they will rear and strike the enemy's mounts and the enemy soldiers as well. They have struck down many an opponent and left a lifeless body. They are well worth twice what I ask. However, if you are not . . ."

Abisha moved away from the wall, and Kiri saw the king's lifted hand, striking silence. Prince Tebmund waited politely.

"Why do you bring them to sell," asked the king, "if they are so fine?"

"Our horses are our living, our finest commodity. We raise them and train them to sell. If you are not interested, there are others who will be. We offered first to you, King Sardira, because we felt that your court, of all the nations, would hold the best and kindest horsemen."

That, thought Kiri, was laying it on pretty thick. Though it had been true once, when Papa was the king's master of horse.

Prince Tebmund said, "I will be more than pleased to give you a fortnight in which your soldiers can work with these four mounts under my direction, to learn their unusual ways. I would not sell them without training men to their skills. If," he said softly, "at the end of that time, you are not pleased with the horses and with the price, I will depart happily with the horses, and no charge made."

Kiri strained to see the king's face. It was set in a scowl, but there was a gleam of interest in his black eyes. A fortnight in which Sardira's captains could learn some interesting secrets about training war-horses, and in which some of the king's own mares might be secretly bred to the two fine stallions. Then, if Sardira didn't buy, he would still have the benefit of a beginning to a fine new line of mounts . . . at no cost. Of course the king would accept. Sardira cared for nothing if not for expediency and self-gain.

Kiri wondered if Prince Tebmund had any idea that horses sold here would soon belong to the dark invaders.

Or perhaps Prince Tebmund didn't care.

King Sardira played both sides. He courted the few leaders who stood valiantly against the dark enemies, and courted the dark invaders with equal favor. They came to Dacia often, seeking supplies and soldiers and whatever else the city could provide. Their flesh lust was easily pandered to in the quarters of the drugged servants and in the stadium fights between prisoners and animals. Those exhibitions sickened and terrified Kiri. The dark unliving wanted whatever new depravity the city and Sardira's court could produce. In return, they offered Sardira flattery and the means for further power through their magic. The unliving were conquerors. They lusted to make war, to kill in battle. They would, when they saw Prince Tebmund's horses, offer Sardira far more than two hundred gold pieces per head, to send such animals into the fighting.

They would let the horses win for them, but they would thirst to see them fight for their lives, see them injured and screaming in pain. Pain and death fed the unliving.

It was the un-men and Sardira together who had cut out her father's tongue, to prevent the images that his voice could bring alive. Their way had been far more cruel than killing him. To silence Colewolf was to sentence him to a cold half death.

Didn't this young prince understand the nature of the dark? Didn't he know that Sardira traded with them? His uncaring ignorance angered Kiri.

Yet why should it? She had no reason to think he was anything more than just another friend of the dark.

Still, if he was a friend of the dark, he could have taken his horses directly to them. His coming to Sardira was just as bad, though. If he was willing to sell his fine, spirited animals to any cruel taker, even where they would be used to help the unliving, he was no better than the dark leaders. It was people like Prince Tebmund, who helped the dark for their own selfish gain, that made the battle so one-sided. She stood shaken with anger, but very aware that she must not lose control.

When Kiri slipped away from the great hall at last, it was all she could do to keep herself in hand. Her inner turmoil frightened her. To let her feelings rule her was too dangerous—for herself and for the cause she served. Why had Prince Tebmund stirred such anger in her?

And the eyes of that black stallion! She could not forget them.

The next morning Kiri was late getting to her cousin Accacia's apartments. She stopped in the servant's scullery to heat the lemon juice and grind the minten leaves she used to wash Accacia's hair, then fled up the six flights to her cousin's floor. Accacia, of course, was in a temper, her brown eyes angry. Kiri supposed she had been pacing; her green satin robe swirled around her as she bore down on Kiri.

"Can't you ever be on time? We have an important visitor in the palace, and I want to look my best—to please Abisha, of course, when he presents me. Do get on now as quickly as you can." She flung herself into the straight satin chair and leaned her head back over the silver tub. Kiri lifted Accacia's long chestnut hair up into the vessel and began to pour on the warm herbed lemon juice. The minten leaves made a fine lather, and soon Accacia relaxed under Kiri's knowing fingers. The hearthfire had been built up to dry Accacia's hair, making the room very hot.

It was an ornate room, not to Kiri's liking. Too much gold-leaf filigree in the screens and furniture, too much crowding of satin draperies over the bed and at the windows, so one had a closed-in feeling. It was a room that couched Accacia's beauty as a velvet-lined box would couch a jewel.

Accacia had ordered long ago that Kiri alone was to wash her hair and perform other small duties for her, but not because she liked Kiri's company or wanted to make a more secure place for her in the palace, or because they had been raised together. Accacia's father had been related to the king, but it was the girls' mothers who had been sisters. Kiri carried none of the king's blood in her veins, she thought with satisfaction. Accacia kept her to do her bidding because she did so like ordering Kiri around, as she always had since they were babies growing up together. Accacia's mother had died at her birth. Her father had been in the king's guard. When he died in battle, Accacia lived with Kiri's family. She had not left the palace after Kiri's father was maimed and sent away. She got herself engaged to Prince Abisha and promptly commandeered two floors of the west tower for her use. Her sympathy was shallow and short-lived when Kiri and Gram were turned out, to take the tiny cottage below the wall. Kiri guessed she ought to be grateful that Accacia had gotten her appointed a minor page. It was safer than trying to find work in the city, and the information Kiri gleaned in the palace was invaluable to those who mattered.

Kiri was so deep in thought as she shampooed away that she was startled and jerked a hank of hair badly when a shrill voice exploded behind her in the doorway. She turned, her ears filled with Accacia's scolding and with the irritating voice of her cousin's friend Roderica, daughter of the present master of horse. Two maids followed Roderica in, bearing curling irons to heat at Accacia's hearth. The two friends liked to have their hair done together so they could gossip in private. Roderica had no maid of her own and used Accacia's freely. The thin, angular girl shrieked and giggled as they discussed the visiting prince.

"Oh, he's beautiful, Accacia! And young—far too young for you, of course. More nearly my age, I would think." Roderica suffered from jealousy of Accacia, for all that they were friends. And no wonder. Accacia, with her long auburn hair and thick lashes framing golden brown eyes was, if nothing else, certainly the most beautiful girl in the palace. She would marry Prince Abisha at year's end in a ceremony that threatened to overshadow even the terrible wars.

"And the horses . . ." Roderica was saying. "Oh, they are lovely horses, but the king haggled over the price—two hundred pieces of gold for each one. I've near heard of such a price. . . ." So Roderica had been listening, too. Roderica might be silly and loud sometimes, but Kiri knew there was another side to her, a puzzling one. She could never tell what Roderica's mood would be and wondered if sometimes she used the drug cadacus, meant for the queen. Roderica spent much of her time with the sick queen and was the crippled woman's only friend. She had been her handmaid since she was a small child and was the only person the queen would now tolerate. Kiri thought Roderica eavesdropped in order to supply the bored queen with palace gossip. Maybe she brought her news of Accacia, too, and whether she still had relations with the king.

"Why would such a handsome prince travel alone?"

Accacia asked. "Why does he not have attendants, some pretty traveling companions? And why did he travel all this way, past dozens of other kingdoms, to sell his horses?" She sighed. "What a terribly dull journey, all that water to cross."

"He came up the Channel of Barter on a lumber barge out of north Thedria," Roderica said. "He came this far, I heard him say, because . . . Oh, I heard them clearly, they were taking tea in the hall and—"

"And you listened from the pantry," Accacia said, smiling.

"Yes," Roderica said without shame. "He came this far because, he said, he thought the king would give his horses the best care."

Accacia laughed. "No one would travel all that way for such a stupid reason."

"But they are very special horses," Roderica said with her typical superiority about horses, because her father was the king's master of horse—though Roderica herself looked like a broken stick on horseback.

"Humph," said Accacia. "They can't be that special. He was fussing around the stable yard at all hours last night, coddling those horses."

"You watched him?"

"I . . . was late coming in." Accacia could see the stable yard clearly from her windows. "He was at it again this morning. Trying to make it look as if those horses are the most valuable things in Tirror—just to keep the price up, of course."

Kiri held her tongue with effort. Accacia cared nothing

for horses, except if they were flashy and could show her off to advantage. Kiri thought Accacia would find a way sooner or later to ride one of Prince Tebmund's mounts. As for Accacia's opinion of Prince Tebmund himself, she was no great judge of character.

Still, there was something about Prince Tebmund, strange and so unsettling that Kiri couldn't decide what she thought.

She knew she was naturally suspicious. Hadn't she grown up spying, purposely suspicious of everyone? Now, when she caught herself siding with Prince Tebmund despite her disapproval of him, that frightened her. It was not comfortable to feel so confused about someone, not comfortable to feel he should be a friend, or as if they had something in common. It was not safe for the cause she served.

Kiri left Accacia's apartments deep in thought, hardly hearing her cousin's final scolding. She went directly to the training field beyond the stables. Keeping to the shadows of the almond grove, she watched the first demonstration of the four Thedrian horses.

She was not allowed in the stables, though she went there anyway. Roderica's father didn't like her critical looks, for they recalled too plainly that Colewolf had had training skills when he was horsemaster that Riconder could never match. She watched Prince Tebmund demonstrate the larger of the two white mares, then one of the stallions. She watched Sardira's sergeants botch the signals and flail as the horses spun and reared. Too soon Prince Tebmund called a halt—

too soon for Kiri, for she was having a fine time. But not soon enough for the red-faced sergeants, nor, Kiri expected, soon enough for the horses, for they seemed well out of sorts with the clumsy riders. She stood in the almond grove for some time after the horses were returned to the stable and the soldiers had gone. Then she slipped away, to her palace duties.

The smell of boiled suppers was rising from the city. Kiri went by back ways to the scullery, where she helped with the vegetables for a while and picked up several interesting tidbits of gossip. She put together a nice meal for Gram and slipped out to tend to the old lady. It was not until the cover of night fell that she left Gram again to take news of Prince Tebmund and his horses where it could reach the few resistance leaders scattered across the city, and then Papa. Papa had worked with the resistance on Dacia for a while, before he went by barge across the sea to Cayub and Edosta to spy there and recruit rebel troops. Kiri guessed the dark had no idea how much a man could do even after his voice was destroyed. Papa would be very interested in Prince Tebmund and his fine war-horses. The rebels should have those horses, not the dark un-men.

Gram had asked a good many questions about the horses, her thin, angled face caught in eager lines and her blue eyes alight with interest. Kiri knew it was hard getting old, having to depend on someone else for exciting new experiences. Gram would rather have seen it all for herself.

Kiri made her way down the twisting lanes, with the stars gleaming in icy brilliance overhead. The cobbles were still warm under her feet, but the wind in from the sea was chill. Voices from the cottages drifted out, some raised in anger. Deeper into the center of the city crude music had begun. She could hear the clink of glasses and smell the sour scent of mithnon as she passed. Here she went quickly, keeping to shadow, her hand on the knife at her thigh. It would be worse later, toward midnight, when gangs began to roam the streets.

It took her almost an hour to cross the city, ever downward along the winding, dropping streets. Finally she came to the stone ruins that stood pale in the starlight, where once had risen a sanctuary of the old and happier civilization. Here, once, all travelers had been welcome. Now, few came, for the dark abhorred this place and had marked the ruins as forbidden. The un-men could not breach the magic of a sanctuary to enter it, but the folk of the city might have entered had not the dark laid a heavy spell to keep them away. Few folk would cross the spell's sense of cold threat, even to save themselves from the dark's mind-rotting evil. The resistance troops crossed, those few humans strong enough, determined enough to fight the dark's powers. The power of the sanctuary helped them keep their minds free.

Animals could always cross the dark's barrier. The speaking animals did not succumb to the wiles of the dark as did humans. They were in perfect tune with the powers of the sanctuary, taking of its strength and protection to help them battle the un-men. Un-men, undead, unliving, the names of the dark were several. Soul buzzards, Kiri thought, for they thirsted after the carrion of men's souls.

Kiri's skin prickled and something cold clutched at her heart as she slipped in among the broken, fallen walls. But the strength of the sanctuary was there, steadying her. She stood for a moment inside, to see that she wasn't followed, before she moved in to where three large stones tilted up to shelter a black hole in the earth. Here she went down on hands and knees.

She slipped down into a hole that had once been part of a larger grotto. Now it was an animal cave, warm and strong-smelling. Here she would give her report about Prince Tebmund and his wonderful horses.

She had no idea what her meager information would finally add up to. She wondered if she wanted to know. Yet regardless of her own misgivings, she knew she must learn more than this. She must seek Prince Tebmund out, perhaps become useful to him in some way so he would talk to her. Kiri's gift, the gift she and her father shared, told her Prince Tebmund was important—either as a friend or as a dangerous foe.

CHAPTER

5

The cave of the great cat was empty. Kiri huddled down inside the door to wait where she could see out across the ruin but remain hidden herself. She could see stars gleaming above the rooftops. She supposed Elmmira was hunting. She had much news for her, for besides the arrival of Prince Tebmund and his horses, there was more frightening information. The dark leaders from the north planned to attack Bukla and Edain very soon, using Dacia as their base. King Sardira would stay in the background as usual, furnishing the dark with troops, horses, food, and weapons forged in his mines. Always seeming neutral, he had recently made a state visit to Edain in the name of friendship. Soon he would destroy Edain.

It had taken Kiri nine long sessions lying on her stomach, pressed into a thin attic space above the king's private chambers, to gather information about the attack. It came by bits and pieces as runners arrived by barge from the neighboring continents, to stand sweating and uneasy in the purple satin room. The king's captains took their orders in his chambers, too, before the blazing fire, sipping mithnon from little amethyst goblets, their voices rising clearly up to Kiri's hiding place.

Kiri sighed with satisfaction, knowing she could tell Elmmira exactly how many troops Quazelzeg expected King Sardira to furnish and how many barges to transport them and the horses across the inlet to Bukla and Edain. She knew where the weapons would be hidden and where grain and fodder had been stored. The most frightening news was that Quazelzeg himself would make his base for the attacks in Sardira's palace. The thought of the dark overlord there in the palace all winter terrified her.

Some of the dark leaders were human men, turned irredeemably to evil. Quazelzeg was not. He was soulless, manlike in shape only, thriving on human degradation. She had watched him twice as she lay in the alcove above the king's ceiling, sick with fear of him. His face had the waxy pallor of too-tight skin drawn over heavy bones. It was a face that never smiled or changed expression. His body was like some terrible machine—colorless and evil. The un-men were not native to Tirror, but had come long ago into this world through the Castle of Doors. They were lured here by a darkness that had spread through Tirror, slowly at first, calling to other evil to come to join it. Quazelzeg came, and the terrors of mind slavery began.

Quazelzeg came here to Dacia sometimes with his

captains for the bloody stadium gaming and to take the favors of the city. His consorts, like Quazelzeg, were chill succubi sucking at the life of the city, drinking in human pain and lust and the suffering of tortured animals.

It was harder for the speaking animals. They had the ability to anticipate the future, like humans, and so they could also anticipate pain and death, whereas the mute animals could not. The speaking animals feared threats to their kin, to their young, and to their human friends.

It was the speaking animals, the great cats and the wolves, who, too often, were pitted against drug-frenzied human prisoners in the stadium games for the entertainment of Quazelzeg and his kind.

Alone in the cave, Kiri frightened herself so much thinking of the bloodless faces of the unliving that she crawled into Elmmira's tangled bed of straw and refuse. She huddled there, shaken and desolate, wishing life could be different, wishing there were no dark invaders and that Papa was home. More than anything, she wished no human would cleave to the darkness, for if they would not, the dark leaders could never win.

She was half asleep when Elmmira came. She leaped up, her knife drawn, before she saw the shape of the great cat against the sky. Elmmira padded in looking smug, with a brace of rabbits dangling and a muffled murmur in greeting. She dropped the rabbits, purred, and rubbed against Kiri.

"You are tense and nervy, Kiri wren. You have been thinking troubled thoughts."

Kiri sheathed her knife, put her arms around Elmmira's silky neck, and pressed her cheek against the great cat's muscled shoulder. Elmmira's warmth was strengthening. Her whiskers scratched Kiri's face, and her muzzle smelled of blood, from the rabbits. Elmmira's rumbling purr shook them both.

"There was good hunting tonight, Kiri wren. Take two rabbits home to your Gram."

"I will," Kiri said gratefully. "We've had no meat in days." The palace kitchen was freer with bread and beans and boiled vegetables than with the fresh meat that the cooks guarded closely. Sometimes Kiri hunted with a bow among the rubble of the city for rabbits or blackbirds, but so did many others, and game was scarce. The great cats were the only hunters who could generally be sure of a meal. They prowled the night-dark streets fading into shadow away from humankind and roamed the rocky coastal cliffs, denning there, taking seabirds. Elmmira's own cave led by secret ways to the sea-cliff dens some quarter mile away, and so to the main part of the ancient sanctuary of Gardel-Cloor. The great cats hunted inland, too, taking wheat rats and hares from the gardens and farms. They lived on Dacia as shadows, moving at night unseen, avoiding with care the traps Sardira sometimes set for them.

Only Kiri and those trusted in the underground could find the cats when they stole away to Gardel-Cloor.

The sanctuary had once been busy with travelers, speaking animals and humans resting together in comfort and warmth. But that was in the old times, the times that could never be again, the times of the singing dragons. There were no singing dragons anymore. When Kiri thought of dragons, she felt as if a part of herself was missing. Yet she had never known dragons, and never would. The dragons were gone from Tirror.

The dragons had held, in their magic, the ultimate powers of the natural world, that world of creatures that knew no corruption. Now the only link between humans and those powers was the speaking animals. Kiri studied Elmmira's gentle bloody paws. Elmmira did not kill for pleasure—no animal did. She killed only for food. There was no evil in the natural world; that was why the dark leaders hated the speaking creatures. Kiri snuggled close to Elmmira's warm side and began to tell her of the invasion plans.

Kiri thought these plans seemed very complete, as if Quazelzeg had engineered this attack more carefully than previous ones. Earlier battles for which King Sardira had furnished troops and supplies had seemed almost haphazard. "As if," Kiri said thoughtfully, "as if now, Quazelzeg is almost uncertain of what he is about. Or uncertain of the outcome."

Elmmira switched her tail and rumbled deep in her throat. "Why should he be uncertain? He will use magic to confuse the peasants of Bukla and Edain. Already he has weakened them, for his disciples have been at work there a long time." She began to lick blood from her paws.

Kiri sighed. "All the same, the planning seems very careful. Could Quazelzeg fear some new threat?"

"What new thing would the dark be afraid of?"

Kiri shook her head. "I don't know." Yet a formless sense of hope touched her. Still, maybe she was only imagining the nervousness and caution that seemed to pervade the dark's messages to King Sardira. "Sometimes," she said, stroking Elmmira's ears, "sometimes I wish I'd been born in ages past, before the dark was so strong. When . . . when there were still dragons."

"Yes," Elmmira said, licking her. "Yes. My poor Kiri."

"Papa . . ." Kiri began, then stopped and pushed the thought away. Papa must wish the same.

"I will take the news of the attack tonight," Elmmira said. She pressed her head against Kiri and placed a heavy, soft paw on her arm. "We do what we can, Kiri wren." She glanced toward the door, her tufted cheeks silhouetted against the starlight. "But you bring more news than Quazelzeg's plans. What is it that excites you so?" She rolled onto her back in one liquid motion and laid her head in Kiri's lap, shaking with purrs as Kiri tickled under her chin.

"There is a prince come to the palace, Elmmira, to sell horses to the king. He brought four by barge from Thedria. And *what* horses! Think of the difference between a farmer's stumpy plow horse and the king's finest charger."

"Not hard to do."

"Now imagine another horse so much more beautiful than the charger, that the charger appears as ugly as a plow pony."

Elmmira's purr thundered louder as she imagined. She squeezed her eyes closed in concentration, then flashed them open. "Horses like that I would like to see."

"Oh, you would be impressed. Fast, strong horses— two black stallions and two white mares. So beautiful. The price is two hundred gold pieces for each. And there are fifty more like them, the prince says, if King Sardira desires."

Elmmira's purring stopped. She licked her shoulder reflectively.

"Prince Tebmund has agreed to remain here," Kiri said, "to train Sardira's troops in the special ways of war the horses have been taught."

"If they are skilled in war, they will help to defeat Bukla and Edain. Does this prince know that? Does he side with the dark?" Elmmira growled softly. "And why, then, has he not taken his offer of such fine horses directly to Quazelzeg?" She rose and began to pace, her tail lashing.

"I don't know why. There's something about him I can't sort out, a feeling. . . . He is wonderful with horses, Elmmira. These horses will strike an enemy mount and even attack enemy soldiers."

"The question is," Elmmira rumbled, "*who* is the enemy to this young prince of Thedria?" The great cat rasped her tongue across Kiri's cheek. "Be careful, Kiri wren. This young prince upsets you."

Kiri shrugged. Elmmira saw her feelings too clearly, just as Gram did. This evening Gram had turned her thin, wrinkled face to Kiri, frowning with the puzzled twist of her mouth and that shrewd look in her eyes. Unlike Elmmira, Gram had said nothing. Gram would bide her time until Kiri felt like talking about it, until Kiri could sort it out in her own mind, whatever the trouble was.

It was late when Kiri made her way back up the twisting, noisy streets carrying the two dead rabbits. Gram was waiting by the hearthfire, worrying as usual. Kiri bolted the door, hugged her, then poked up the fire to warm the cold evening tea. They sat cozily, Gram rocking gently, not talking. Gram's long, bony hands were busy carding wool from a hank she had traded honey for—Kiri had collected the honey south of the city in the loft of an abandoned barn. The veins of Gram's hands were even darker in the shadowing candlelight. She watched Kiri crumble her seedcake, and when she spoke her voice was gravelly with the night's chill. Kiri handed her her scarf to wrap around her throat.

"You're all atangle. Flighty." She said it without criticism. "Is Elmmira all right?"

"Oh, yes. Well, maybe she was edgy. She didn't say anything." She looked up at Gram. "What is it? What have you heard?" For Gram was edgy, too, her bright blue eyes filled with unease.

"There are more traps out. Along the alleys, in the fields. Sardira wants speaking animals for the stadium games. A rag woman told of it; she saw them setting the traps."

"If I could have warned her . . ." Kiri said. "You must have heard it after I left."

Gram nodded. "You'd gone. I was filling the water jugs." Gram often heard useful bits of information among their neighbors. She talked little and listened carefully, and people told her a good deal.

Kiri made a silent prayer for Elmmira. But Elmmira was wary. She could smell a trap—she said it smelled like Sardira's soldiers. Kiri shivered all the same. Maybe she could learn where the traps were set, in which alleys, if she soft-talked one of the stable grooms.

Maybe she could spring those hidden snares with a stick. That was what Papa would do.

Where was Papa tonight?

Perhaps in some secret cellar meeting with others of the underground. Or maybe he was in a street tavern, pretending to be drunk, listening to the loose talk of drunken soldiers. Kiri closed her eyes and tried to see in the special way she and her father had. She could imagine his face, his high, angled cheekbones and square jaw, the laugh lines that made deep curves to frame his mouth . . . that silent mouth bereft of speech. She could see his face, but she could bring no real presence of him this night.

Sometimes if their powers were very strong, and the powers of the dark relaxed, she could sense his thoughts and give him of her own. That was next best to really being with him, to riding together or practicing with bow and sword in the privacy of the ruins as they used to do. That was before Sardira branded her father a traitor and imprisoned and tortured him. Sardira set her father free but mute, thinking he would serve as example to others who fought for freedom. Thinking that Colewolf would be useless, with the voice of the bard taken from him.

They had tied him to a table—it had taken seven men to do that—and cut the tongue from his mouth. He had come home to lie white and shaken on his cot, spitting blood into a basin. There was little Gram could do for him; make him broth, grind salves. His mouth had healed eventually, but his spirit had not. It was after this that he told Kiri, with messages he wrote on a slate and with Gram's help, the truth of her inheritance, that they bore the blood of the dragonbards. He told her with a touching sadness that there were no more dragons and perhaps no more bards than the tiny handful in Dacia. He wrote with great care the meaning that this inheritance had once held, when the dragons lived. With the coming of the dark, then the disappearance of dragons, man's memory had been nearly destroyed, his experience wiped away. Without memory and experience, one had no free choice, for what was there to choose?

Only a few people, strong enough to resist the spells and drugs of the dark, retained their freedom and fought back. But even their numbers were dwindling. "One day," Gram said, "maybe the dragons will return. Then the bards will sing with them; then the sleeping peoples will awaken. Oh, it could happen." The old woman never lost hope. No evil was so terrible that Gram no longer had hope.

Gram poured out the last of the tea and added a dollop of honey, then put her arm around Kiri. Kiri leaned her head on Gram's bony shoulder. Gram's shapeless linen gown smelled of lye soap. Her thin brown-splotched hands were still.

Kiri sighed. "I guess I miss Papa tonight."

"He misses you. He's proud of you, Kiri, and of the work you do." She held Kiri away and looked at her. "The underground needs you, Kiri, just as it needs Colewolf. You are together in this."

There were other spies, of course. Two in the palace, and a dozen or so in the city.

"Every spy is important, Kiri. But the dragonbards—you and Colewolf are symbols of the power that once linked us all."

Kiri nodded. Her tears came suddenly, and she felt ashamed. Papa didn't cry. Why should she?

"War brings forth strange talents," Gram said softly. "It brings forth strange feelings, too." The old woman hugged her, hard. "Come, tell me more about the wonderful horses of Prince Tebmund. I would like to see them working on the training field."

"Oh, Gram, they are wonders." Kiri wiped away her tears, sniffing. "I've never seen such horses. They will rear and strike an enemy on command, will back and kick, and know all kinds of surprising war tricks. If you will wear your warm shawl, I'll take you to watch them. You'll laugh at Sardira's soldiers trying to keep their seats."

"You should be riding such horses, not the king's clumsy troops. Another talent," Gram said, touching Kiri's hand, "another talent that will one day know its own."

It was not until Kiri lay snuggled in bed beneath her thick quilt, leaving Gram nodding beside the fire, that she wondered. What *would* this war bring forth in herself? What might it force her to discover about herself? Not about the child Kiri, or the woman-to-be Kiri, but about the other, secret Kiri whom she hardly knew—the bard. The one who sang sometimes to the speaking beasts. The Kiri who had such terrible yearnings for a freedom and power that would never be and that she only half understood.

Kiri had made Colewolf smile with pleasure when she sang at the last rebel meeting four months ago in the secret underground cavern of Gardel-Cloor. She had made a small song to bring alive times past—had made whispers echo in the cavern—and the nebulous shadows of people a long time dead.

If she had been paired with a dragon, the shadows

would have come to life, blazing into real figures, the voices rung out strongly, the passions and desires of generations become real. But she was only half a power, alone and incomplete. She sighed. She was gifted, yes. Gram forever reminded her that she had special gifts. But what good were they, alone?

There were, in all the world of Tirror as far as Kiri knew, only two other bards besides herself and her father. There was golden-haired Summer, with eyes like the sea. She was a capable spy and had gone as servant in the household of the dark leader Vurbane, on Ekthuma. From there, Summer sent messages home about the movement of the dark armies, about weapons stores and supplies. Summer, too, felt an emptiness because she was dragonbard-born, in a world without dragons.

The other bard was seven-year-old Marshy. Garit and a handful of resistance soldiers had found him as a baby, abandoned in a muddy slew. Little crippled Marshy would not believe there were no more dragons. He insisted on singing his clear-voiced songs that made hazy images of children long vanished, and tore at Kiri's heart. He spoke of the singing dragons as if one day they would come and lift Tirror out of war. But Marshy was only a little boy and still a terrible dreamer.

What good did it do that there were four bards, when there were no dragons?

Her singing had pleased the troops, though. Maybe it had lightened their spirits. But her powers could wane so quickly. They seemed strongest in the grotto of Gardel-Cloor. Elsewhere on Dacia, the murky confusion the dark laid down was too powerful for her. Then she had only her own eyes and ears and quick feet to help her. She had not even the dimpled smile and naughty eyes of Accacia with which to win people's confidence. If she had Accacia's looks, she could be the cleverest spy in all Tirror. And what did Accacia do with her beauty? Nothing of value, only that which brought favors, diamonds, velvet gowns, and the most luxurious apartments in the west tower. Kiri sighed. If she had half Accacia's looks, she could learn quickly enough all about Prince Tebmund.

Well, the first thing to do was take Gram to watch his horses. If he saw her and Gram admiring them, it would be easier to get acquainted.

Kiri and Gram woke to a foggy morning, the rooftops and streets below them smothered in white, the black towers above half hidden. They made their way through the back halls of the palace and behind the stables, beneath the windows of the horsemaster's apartments, then into the dim almond grove. Across the gaming field, the black stone pergola that housed the king's viewing box was filled with soldiers and palace guards and ladies. Kiri could see the black-robed king seated in his tall carved chair. All along the stone wall that divided the field from the stables, grooms and pages stood watching. The horsemaster watched from the gate. Kiri made Gram comfortable with the blanket.

The old woman sat entranced as Prince Tebmund galloped the white mare in circles, then with a touch made her run backward. They watched her rear on command and strike out, wheel and kick, duck and drop down crouching as if evading a sword. Kiri longed to have one chance at such a horse and knew Gram felt the same.

When the three mounted soldiers began to try war maneuvers, Gram shook her head. The horses outturned them and outthought them, yet these men were powerful horse soldiers. Kiri took fine delight in their awkwardness. Gram stared at them with scorn, but her eyes filled with pleasure at the horses and her old hands twitched, yearning to hold the reins. She had been a fine horsewoman in her day. Kiri had brought an image of her once, in a small song sung in privacy and easier to do than bringing a whole city alive. It was of Gram as a young girl, riding a great piebald stallion over hurdles.

They walked home slowly, Kiri awash with regret that the eager old woman was now trapped in that frail, aging body. She wished she could give Gram one wonderful ride on those magical horses. The high road was crowded now, with folk herding sheep and goats, some begging, a few driving loaded carts to the palace kitchens. At home, she settled Gram by the wood stove and heated soup for her, then went out again to tend to Accacia. But when she started up the high road she saw Prince Tebmund on the white mare coming toward her between carts, the foot traffic making way for him.

She ducked in behind some cottages, then wondered at her own timidity. She peered out, unnerved, as he wheeled the mare lightly and trotted back toward the palace. She had botched the perfect opportunity.

She watched him ride through the palace gate, furious at herself. She could not have found a better way to meet Prince Tebmund than here among crowds where it would seem an accident. She had ruined it with her unaccountable, gawking shyness.

CHAPTER
6

Sour, Seastrider said, staring at the faces they passed along the road. *Don't they know how to smile?*

They haven't much to smile about, Teb said as they turned in through the palace gate. *The girl was smiling, the page. She went between the cottages back there, the girl who was watching us from the almond grove, the one you find so interesting.*

The one you *find interesting, Tebriel. The girl we just followed down the high road because* you *wanted to speak to her.* Seastrider switched her tail. *You already know her name is Kiri. She and that old woman know how to admire a horse, all right. But you have learned little else about her.*

Only that she is cousin to Accacia, and that her father was once horsemaster in this palace. Perhaps that is what we see in her, a sympathy and knowledge of fine mounts.

Perhaps, Tebriel.

But what else? Could she be one for whom we search?

I do not know, Tebriel. She bears watching. And what of last night's venture? Didn't you see her then?

If you know my thoughts, why do you ask me?

They are not clear. Nothing comes clear in this dark-ridden place.

I learned little in the city. Twice I fought off drugged gangs. People were closemouthed, or too drugged to make sense. As I was coming back up the hill I saw candlelight suddenly where the cottage door opened, saw a girl's figure. It was very dim, but was in the place where her cottage stands. It might have been Kiri. It was near midnight—strange for a young woman to be about so late in this cursed city. You are right, as usual. She interests me. I mean to find out why.

They turned into the stable yard and Teb slid down, waving a groom away. He stripped off the saddle and halter, gave Seastrider a quick rubdown and fresh water, then slapped her on the rump. *Go and play; go eat grass.* She twitched her ears at him, then wheeled away through the side gate and sped for the far hills, where her brothers and sister were grazing. The groom stared after her unbelieving. But he'd had his instructions. Teb stood watching them, thinking idly that the horsemaster, Riconder, had been somewhat reserved in his admiration. *Jealous,* Seastrider had said, and didn't like the man. This could pose a problem they hadn't counted on. Well, no matter; the king was impressed enough. Teb turned reluctantly back to the palace, where the king awaited him.

There seemed to be a lot of social ritual—state

breakfasts and morning tea with the king, a lot of dressing up. It was difficult to slip away into the city. He had expected ritual, but not so early in the day. He yawned, and thought of stealing up to his chambers for a short nap. He'd had little sleep the night before, returning from the taverns of the city to toss restlessly. He had gone well armed and was glad of that, had changed some of his gold into the local silver reppets stamped with Sardira's profile. He had learned little of importance, but there was a candle shop open quite late, with an unusual amount of traffic, and that would bear watching. The night before that, his first night in Dacia, he had escaped to the horses, then to the sky, as soon as the palace darkened. He had clung to Seastrider's back, shouting into the wind with pent-up frustration at fancy palace ceremonies.

They had invaded the island of Felwen with their song and had caused three dark leaders to be hanged from the manor house belfry. Teb smiled. It wouldn't be a bad stay in Dacia if they could escape every few nights to some action. He didn't think he was cut out to play the part of a palace dandy.

Well, but he must. He must be courtly and smile and try to remember his manners.

That night, when palace windows darkened, they were off again, this time over Wintrel, where the dragons could sense an evil sabbath in progress long before they sighted the island.

It was a dance of hate. A circle of fires burned, and within danced twenty young girls, chained and naked, forced to dance, prodded by pokers when they faltered. Teb could feel the dark leader's elation and knew he took strength from the girls' fear and pain. Yesod had dressed himself in the skin of a goat, the horns bound to his forehead. His ugly laugh was cruel and cold, his eyes flashing with hungry lust.

There were no woods on Wintrel. The dragons wove themselves in among the boulders that lined its western shore. Teb climbed the rocks and stared off north to the ring of ritual fires. The music was pagan and invasive and made evil thoughts come in him, so he welcomed Seastrider's nudge and moved close to her great flat cheek as they began to sing.

Slowly Teb and the dragons countered the pagan music, weakened its force. Yesod and his four consorts began to fidget. Teb watched the girls' faces, saw them brighten. They began to fight their chains.

But then Yesod's power increased. The girls cowered, and knelt in worship of Yesod. The dark leader smiled, a leer as cold as winter. Teb and the dragons tried to bring their powers stronger, but their images of freedom and dignity shattered. They watched Wintrel's people drop back into lethargy. The power of this dark leader was too great. Teb was riven with fear of what Yesod could do—of what he *would* do to Tirror, now that he knew there were dragons.

Now, they must make sure that he died.

We must bring Yesod here to us, Seastrider said. *It is the only way to destroy him. We must call him to us with twisted images.*

It was not easy to use their powers to call forth evil. Teb sang of a dark time, of dark creatures, for all history was a part of the dragon song. Yesod listened to that song. He began to approach the dark images, moving mechanically. The tangle of sirens and lamias and snake-tailed basilisks drew him to them. He held out his hands to the twisting shadows but looked beyond them at Teb and the dragons.

He knew they were singing, knew they were luring him, yet he came on, embracing the dark mimicries that flowed around him, wanting them with a lust for evil that drugged reason. Teb's blood went cold with fear of him.

Yesod approached the cliff, fondled by the evil creatures. They led him with lurid gestures, with thoughts so bloody he didn't care that they were only shades. He reached toward the cliff, thirsting for the dark songs, sucking on them. His disciples followed him. The dark images moved over the crest of the cliff and down it toward the sea, spinning titillating sensations like steel scarves to draw the dark leaders.

The dark masters stepped out into air. They fell. Yesod screamed once.

They lay below, twisted on the sharp stone, dying. The sea's tides would take them, then the sharks. Teb thanked the Graven Light that the un-men, evil as they were, still could die. They *were* the dark side of mortal, he guessed—the black mirror image of what mankind should be.

The killing sickened Teb, but there was no alternative. Each night, as more folk were freed, Teb could only hope they would remain so and take up arms to join with the resistance.

But that was their decision. Teb and the dragons could win their freedom for them but could not choose what they would do with it.

He must find a way to the underground soon. Maybe he could help bring the newly freed peoples into it, if they wanted to fight the dark. No one in the palace had given any sign that they worked with the rebels. There had been no plying questions to try to find out Teb's own sympathies. Accacia's coy questions added up to nothing yet. He followed her the next night— or thought he did—a dark, full-skirted shadow slipping deep into the palace passages. He discovered when she lit a lamp that it was not Accacia, but her friend Roderica, the thin, graceless horsemaster's daughter. Teb followed her on through dark, twisting ways to an ironclad door.

He watched her unlock it and slip inside, leaving the door ajar, the soft light of the room spilling into the passage. He could see the end of a bed with rumpled blankets but could not tell if someone was in it. He was about to move closer when Roderica reappeared carrying a tray and set it down on the floor of the passage as if meaning for servants to retrieve it. It contained a bowl and mug. The bowl was half full of something pasty like cold porridge, half a small meat pie, and a peach seed. Roderica retreated and closed the door, leaving him in darkness. He waited for perhaps an hour before light spilled out again. He had pressed against the door to listen but could hear only the blurred hum of two women's voices. When Roderica came out, he was back in the shadows. As she paused, the raspy woman's voice from inside complained.

". . . porridge. I'm sick to death of porridge."

"I'll tell them," Roderica said. "Stewed chicken and gravy, and no porridge." She locked the door and pocketed the key.

Teb followed her lantern light back through the dark passages, committing the way to memory, remembering his glimpse of the locked room, remembering the old, cracked voice of the woman. The service on the tray had been of gold, with embroidered linen. The bed frame had been ornate, the carpet rich. But the door was kept locked.

He began to listen more carefully at the interminable state meals and functions for mention of the prisoner. He gleaned no information. He took himself down into the city, among the taverns and brothels late at night, to listen to gossip. He had found that if he dined with the king and lingered politely afterward, he was soon released to spend the rest of the evening as he chose.

Seastrider would not let him go alone this time. She took the shape of a great gray wolf with some difficulty, not a speaking wolf but a wild, roving wolf such as she sensed in a small band on the black mountain. Teb went among the city flanked by a natural killer. Though they were watched and followed, no one came close to him. He asked oblique questions, lounging at tables dressed in his old, stained leathers, and drank too much mithnon, for which he was sorry the next day. He learned little of real interest and felt stifled and shamed by the sick townsfolk stinking of drugs. The white powdered cadacus was easy to come by, and he was stared at strangely when he refused it.

No man would speak against the king, or against the dark leaders from the north, though one old man said, glancing around him with caution, "*They* aren't afraid of the dark ones. *They* hide things from them. . . ." But when Teb tried to learn who *they* were, the old leather-faced man took panic and fled the tavern. Teb dared not follow; too many eyes were watching.

He learned nothing about the palace page, Kiri, on these night visits. He saw little of her until the morning she stood watching him from an alley that led off the main palace courtyard.

He had been talking with Prince Abisha. He left him as quickly as he could to follow her, but she had disappeared. He saw her again two days later as he left his chambers, her face dull and without expression but her dark eyes very alive before she turned away quickly through a side door. The door seemed a private one. He didn't follow her. Then one afternoon he saw her in the city, trading for candles at the shop he had been watching.

It was a tiny building made of rough boards set against two walls of a stone ruin. It sold only candles, yet its customers seemed many for such a place, and most of them strong young people. Kiri went in carrying a string bag. He could see her bartering a clay crock for candles. He stayed in the tavern across the way, beside its small open window. When she came out, a mob of roving boys no more than twelve were lounging around a small horse corral attached to the tavern. They saw Kiri alone and, moving quickly, were around her, striking at the heavy string bag with sticks, and then at her legs and arms. Teb left through the window. He gathered four of them by their dirty collars. The other three fled up the muddy lane. Kiri stood gawking at him.

She was not in her page's tunic but in dirty rags, her face smeared with dirt, her feet bare. The two crocks in the string bag, those she had not traded, were broken. Thick globs of golden honey ran down through the mesh to puddle in the muddy street. Teb saw the knife in her hand and knew without her saying that she had been loath to use it on such children. She saw him looking at it and, with no false modesty, lifted her skirt and slipped it into the sheath tied against her leg.

"Children," he said. "But they meant to hurt you."

She nodded. "Thank you. I would have had to hurt them."

"Yes."

She looked down at the string bag, then emptied it into the gutter, retrieving a dozen stubby candles first, staring with regret at the pieces of broken crock scattered in the honey and mud. "Gram's good crocks. She had them a long time."

"Are you going back to the palace? I will walk with you."

Above them, as they climbed, the rising hills with their crowded houses and stone ruins were all in shadow. The high ridge of the mountain above the black castle flared red with the setting sun. The smell of a hundred suppers cooking mixed with the smell of soggy animal pens.

Teb said, "He does quite a business, that candlemaker."

"He makes the best candles in Dacia."

Teb studied her. "It seems strange that his customers are all so . . . they're all healthy young people."

Her brown eyes were steady, her face lean and alert. She shook her head. "I don't think that's strange. That shop is the only one in Dacia where you can get candles that aren't tallow. These candles are beeswax. Tallow candles make people cough." She smiled at him. "I bring the candlemaker beeswax, along with my honey."

He looked at her closely. "All you get for your wax and honey are a few candles in trade?"

"Oh, no." She dug in her pocket and brought out a handful of small silver reppets with the face of Sardira on each. Teb looked at the coins and studied her solemn, innocent face. His good sense told him the candle shop was a meeting place. He wished he knew Kiri better. He would go back there. If the shop *was* such a place, and if Garit was in Dacia, then Garit might appear there sooner or later.

Teb got no real information out of Kiri. She was clever at fencing his questions. He was increasingly interested in that skill.

He left her at her door, meaning to talk with her again soon. Meantime there were other answers he wanted. He wanted to know more about the ugly games in the stadium, and whether captured rebel soldiers were tortured as a part of the entertainment. He wanted to know how many dark leaders came to Dacia for the games.

CHAPTER

7

"You have told me little of the stadium games," Teb said, watching Accacia. "We have nothing like them in Thedria. There must be huge crowds, visiting dignitaries?" He busied himself breaking bread, served with the first course, of shellfish. "Are such games enjoyed often, or only on special occasions?"

"Oh, special occasions," Accacia said brightly. "When the leaders of the north come," she said, delicately forking a river clam from its shell. "When they come, there is gaming at night in the stadium and feasting, and slaves will dance in all the taverns." Her golden-brown eyes were bright with excitement.

He sipped at the pale wine. "What kind of contests? Men against men, or against animals?"

"All kinds, giant cats battling wolves, or both driven to attack chained prisoners." Her color rose with lust.

"Prisoners?" he asked casually.

"Enemies of the king, and of Dacia. There are wild horses, too, battling with drugged bulls. Only not any horses like yours, Prince Tebmund. Once," Accacia said, tossing her chestnut hair, "once there was a unicorn brought from the lands beyond the sea, trussed up, and sold to King Sardira. It fought the king's brown guard lizards all alone until it bled to death."

Teb clenched his jaws, watching her, sickened. Unicorns were rare creatures, never seen on these lands anymore, though their pictures were painted on the walls of the ancient sanctuaries. Rare and valued creatures—if one had any sense of value. The king's guard lizards were as big as horses, with triple rows of razor-sharp teeth and claws, as long as his hand, like sharp curved knives. The king had shown him two, his first day in the palace, pointing them out from a slit window, where the lizards paced in a small inner court.

Accacia's knee brushed his leg, and the candlelight shone on her hair. Teb wanted to ask more about the prisoners, the enemies of the king. But Abisha across from him heard every word, though the pale, flabby man ate methodically with no change of expression, except an occasional small frown at his fiancée. Teb didn't dare ask outright how many dark leaders came here, or who they were.

The king was watching him, too, whether because of his questions about the games or because Accacia was leaning too close to him, smiling too much, Teb wasn't sure.

But it was not only the king's stare or Accacia's too warm attention that made Teb edgy. There was something else, something beyond this table, a presence or a force that stirred in him a sharp pang of unease. This was not the first time he had felt it. It touched him like a cold hand, then vanished. A dark threat, telling him to beware.

Roast lamb was being served and trenchers of vegetables and warm, fragrant breads. Teb fell to with enthusiasm. For nearly five years in Nightpool he had lived on nothing but fish and shellfish—raw at first, then cooked inexpertly by his own hand. And before that, there were four years of dry bread and table scraps when he was prisoner in his murdered father's palace. He wished now he could simply enjoy the wonderful food and not have to try to work information from a woman who, too obviously, had more intimate things in mind, and who drew the eyes of both king and prince to him too critically.

"It is a fine dining hall," he said, speaking up table to the king, "beautifully appointed, and the food is superior. I would guess there is no grander hall or fare anywhere on Tirror."

The king smiled. "The carvings are from the eastern mountains of the Reinhollen dwarves, brought by barge when my father ruled. The jewels were dug from our own mines, of course, as jewels are dug, still, by my slaves."

It surprised Teb that the king's father would still be mentioned, that any tradition was spoken of here. Wherever the dark insinuated itself into the land, the past was wiped from the memory of men, or at least from their conversation and caring. He studied the hall. Its ornate, crowded, heavily carved panels were more oppressive than beautiful. The mountain's black stone at the back lost itself in its own shadows, except where water dripped out from underground springs, catching the candlelight. Teb thought of another hall, his home in Auric, with walls of the palest masonry and banks of windows. There, sunlight seemed always to touch his mother's face, and bright tapestries hung everywhere.

By the time he was twelve the tapestries were gray and tattered, the palace a dismal, smelly camp for Sivich's soldiers. His mother was gone. His father was dead, and he and his sister, Camery, slaves to Sivich, his father's killer. He was startled when Accacia leaned over his arm.

"You must see the city for yourself, Prince Tebmund. There will be no entertainment tomorrow, but I can show you Dacia. We can ride out early in the morning if you like, and—"

"A party to view the city," Prince Abisha interrupted. His look at his fiancée was cold and knowing. "A fine idea. I will arrange it. But not tomorrow. Grain and stores will be shipped tomorrow. The streets will be jammed with carts. The next day, perhaps. We shall see."

She glared, then retreated into an icy smile. "Directly after breakfast would be best, while it is still cool."

Abisha didn't bother to answer her. He signaled for more roast lamb.

Teb thought in the morning he would take his mounted trainees down into the city on the excuse of giving them experience on crowded streets. . . . It would be some action, something different, and he might see something of value. He itched to be away from the supper table and up above the earth looking down between Seastrider's wings. He hated waiting each night until the whole palace slept.

It was bad luck he had been assigned rooms just below Accacia's apartments and that she could see the stable from her windows. It was interesting that she had made mention of it this evening as he accompanied her into the dining hall. But there was no law against his going to the stable, or against riding at night.

"Do you not have stone carvers in Thedria?" the king was asking.

"No. No dwarfs of any kind, nor have I ever seen one," Teb said truthfully. He could answer that kind of question. The history of Tirror's peoples was a part of all dragon-song lore. It was questions about small new customs that worried him and that could draw wrong answers.

"Then how do you decorate your palaces? And what pastimes, Prince Tebmund, do the folk of Thedria find appealing? Do you not have stadium games?"

Teb laughed. "I'm afraid our two palaces are mostly rough and undecorated, King Sardira. And as for pastimes, I suppose our folk have little time to pass in recreation. They farm and fish, and even those of the palace find common work to do when they are not working with the colts. I'm afraid you would find us a dull lot in Thedria, quite unable to offer such luxuries as this grand banquet, or such entertainment as your stadium games."

It seemed forever to Teb before he was alone in his chambers. He pulled off his fancy clothes and changed to his leather trousers and tunic, folding the stolen clothes over a silver clothes stand. The red wool was soft, very like a red dress his mother had worn. Red was her favorite color. A picture of her filled his mind; she was dressed in red, her silhouette sharp against a red tapestry as she turned to look out her chamber window, the sun full on her face.

She seemed to him, now, so much more than his mother. He knew only that she traveled in worlds beyond Tirror, searching for her own dragon mate. As a child he had not known, nor would have understood, her need, though he had felt that she yearned for something, something secret and wild that she would not share with him and Camery. It left him puzzled and excited.

He and his mother and Camery were all flung apart now, so they might never see each other again. He hoped it had been Camery whom Nightraider sensed there on that small island. He could see her in memory, a skinny little girl riding pell-mell down the meadows on her fat bay pony, her knees tucked in and her pale hair flying; he could hear her laughter when she beat him in a race, and see her green-eyed scowl when she didn't.

He paced his chamber, avoiding the heavy furniture, watching the palace wings through his velvet-draped windows. How long it took for all the windows to darken and the palace to sleep. The wind was rising. He could feel Seastrider's impatience on the dark hills as the white mare snorted and pawed.

He guessed he didn't take much to court life. He'd lived too long in his simple cave among the otters of Nightpool, and then in the dragon lair. He guessed animals were more open in their dealings than humans, not so impressed with ritual. The animals had ritual, too, but of a simpler kind. The foxes of the caves of Nison-Serth had their family rituals, but they were gentle, loving ones, like bathing together in the household pool.

The otters' rituals had been more complicated. But they were directly connected with council meetings, not used for vanity, nor as background for mating, which the otter families handled more directly. Teb was not without desire for women, but he didn't much like complicated flirting, particularly when it concerned Accacia's meaningful glances.

She had come to his door last night very late because, she said, she heard noises on the stair. He had pointed out to her that if the noises were on the stair, she would have been safer behind her own bolted door. She had flashed him a look of cold anger and left quickly, her blue robe swirling around her ankles.

He wondered if her flirting was a cover, if she might

be a contact with the underground, wanting to learn his true mission. She had given no hint of that. She could be just what she seemed, a little tart. He would hold his judgment and see where the flirting led. Seastrider thought her a common trollop. Seastrider had decided opinions. Well, that was the nature of dragons.

Seastrider's comments about the soldiers who rode her weren't flattering, either. All four dragons were hard put not to buck off their heavy-handed riders. It was difficult enough, they said, to hold the shape shifting for such long times without having to put up with the Dacian soldiers jerking their halters and kicking them. Teb did not point out to them that it was *their* idea to come here. He had a hard time convincing the Dacian soldiers, too, that these horses did not need bits in their mouths and would not tolerate spurs.

He thought how Garit would have ridden them, gentle-handed and wise, understanding at once their perceptiveness. Garit had stayed on as horsemaster after Teb's father was murdered, serving the dark leader, Sivich, and certainly hating him. He had stayed to help Teb and Camery when the chance finally came. When Sivich's men discovered there was still a singing dragon on Tirror, Sivich decided to capture it, using Teb as bait. It was the small birthmark on Teb's arm that told Sivich he was a dragonbard.

Sivich had been an ignorant fool to think that a singing dragon would let itself be captured. Teb supposed that in his embarrassment at failure Sivich had kept the fact that there was a dragon again on Tirror a secret. Maybe he still dreamed of trapping her. He was a fool as well as an incredibly evil man. He followed the dark leaders eagerly. It was Sivich's kind, more than any other, that helped the dark grow strong. Teb intended that Sivich would die painfully and slowly for the murder of his father.

Garit had outsmarted Sivich handily when he freed Teb from Sivich's army before they reached the site of the dragon trap. Garit fled on horseback to lead Sivich's soldiers away from Teb, where he hid in the sanctuary of Nison-Serth. Garit didn't know Teb had been captured a second time and chained in the dragon snare. Surely it was Garit who had returned to Auric much later, to the tower, to free Camery. The great owl, Red Unat, winging across the channel to Nightpool, had brought Teb news that she was gone.

Teb began to pace again, impatient to join the dragons. He wondered—if he could bring folk awake, he and Seastrider, make folk cast off the mind-numbing dark, maybe he could make them sleep, too.

Half amused, he tried a song of peace, singing softly, his voice moving out onto the night breeze too quietly to be consciously heard through open windows. The song came to him easily, and he felt more power than he should; then he realized Seastrider was singing with him, a whisper of dragon song. They wove a subtle ballad filled with stars and soft winds, and pretty soon the palace lights began to be snuffed, one here, two there. The reflections of light from the rooms below him began to die.

At last the night was black, with only the stars for light. Teb slipped out his chamber door, to the shadows of hall and stair.

CHAPTER

8

The white mares were silhouetted against the night, the two black stallions visible only because they hid the stars. Teb swung onto Seastrider's back. They headed at a fast trot for the hills. "We made good magic," he said. "The palace sleeps soundly."

"It was not our magic alone, Tebriel. There is power around us tonight. There is something in the palace of bright power. Can't you feel it?"

"What kind of something? I can sense only the dark."

"I don't know what it is." Seastrider tossed her head. "I expect you will be aware of it, given time . . . and a little freedom to breathe, among all the social complications of these humans."

So she had sensed his frustration at the supper table. "Are you laughing at me?"

She didn't answer but broke into a gallop, the other three beside her, and they headed for the far hills.

Once out of sight of the palace, they let their horse shapes slide away, and the four dragons burst skyward on the cold west wind. They swept out over the black sea, banking and gliding, spending their pent-up, restless passion in a storm of spinning flight.

When they settled at last, they dove for shark, Teb half-drowned as usual, his ears full of water and his boots full as well. On an outcropping rock the dragons made their meal. When they took to the sky once more, still possessed by wildness, Teb clung, dizzy and laughing. The lands below them were all dark, not a light anywhere. The sea heaved with patches of phosphorescence so it was brighter than the land-world. Against the shores, white waves broke.

They did not touch any country this night. They dove low, observing, sensing the dark. There was strong evil on Liedref. They picked out half a dozen other lands where they would return to battle the dark invaders. As dawn neared, the dragons made for Dacia, swooping low over the small continents that bordered the Sea of Igness. They came down over Dacia to the west, behind the mountain that held the palace. They could see the mountain's wild western face where trees twisted between giant boulders. They hovered there listening, but there was no sound.

They made for the gentler hills, where the dragons shifted shape and trotted back docilely to the palace stables. Teb's boots squinched seawater when he dismounted.

It was that morning that Teb, prompted by Accacia's remarks, thought again of the locked door in the dark palace passage, where an old woman's cracked voice had complained, ". . . porridge. I'm sick to death of porridge."

Roderica had taken breakfast at the king's table with her father. The horsemaster, Riconder, a square, silent man with a look of resentment about him, spoke little to Teb. He praised the horses, it seemed, only out of duty. When he rose, his daughter followed him, and Accacia, clinging to Teb's arm, giggled. "Don't be late with your ward's breakfast, Roderica."

Teb had a quick vision of Roderica going down the dark hall carrying a lamp, unlocking that lonely, heavy door.

"And don't forget the queen's porridge," Accacia said rudely. "She does so love her cold porridge."

The queen.

Teb hadn't known there was a queen, had supposed her long dead. He glanced at the king, who had risen, and saw no change of expression. He made an excuse as soon and as deftly as he could and left Accacia. He hurried down the dark passage until he saw Roderica ahead, her lamp casting a swaying light up the dark walls. She approached a passage where brighter lamps burned. He stopped and drew back into blackness as she flung open double doors.

It was the kitchen inside; he could hear the clanging of utensils and smell food and dishwater. She came out, followed by a page boy carrying a breakfast tray. Teb waited until they had rounded a bend, then followed. He waited again while the food was delivered beyond the oak door. When the page had left, he settled against the wall. He had no time to move away when Roderica came out quickly, straight for him, and grabbed his arm.

She was a thin girl, tall, with an angled face, sour and unsmiling. "Why did you follow me? I have no use for spies, even if you are a prince."

"I would like to visit the queen."

"Why? No one visits her."

"That's why." He thought the best approach was the direct one. Roderica seemed serious now, without the frivolity she displayed at other times. A strange girl, changeable and confusing.

"I didn't know there was a queen," Teb told her. "I thought her long dead. I am curious. Is there any harm in that?"

She looked him over, not speaking, holding the lamp high so her own face fell into angled shadows.

"Isn't she lonely? Wouldn't she like a visitor?"

"She has me. I am all she needs. The king would be furious if he knew you were here."

"Do you mean to tell him?"

At that moment the door flew open and the old woman stood leaning against the sill. "What is it, Roderica? Who are you talking to? Bring him in here."

She was dressed in a pale pink dressing gown with quantities of ruffles, an old gray sweater pulled over it. Her feet were shod in heavy sheepskin slippers. Her white hair flew wildly around her thin, wrinkled face. She leaned heavily on the doorframe as Roderica reached for her, then nearly fell as the young woman steadied and turned her toward the bed. Teb followed them into the room.

When she was ensconced at last under the tumbled blankets, she fixed her faded blue eyes on Teb. "Well? Who is he, Roderica? Why did you bring him here?"

"I didn't. He followed me. He is a prince of Thedria, selling horses."

The old woman's laugh ended with coughing. "I do not buy horses, young man. I am past that."

"I came *here* out of curiosity. Why do they lock you up?"

"The king locks me up. He has no longer any use for me. He finds my weakness and infirmities unpleasant. I am content here with my own company. As you can see, it is a comfortable chamber. I do not have to make any decisions here, or be civil to visitors."

It *was* an opulent chamber, but windowless, one of the rooms dug from the side of the mountain. He didn't know how anyone could stand to be so trapped. He studied her pale blue eyes, faded to white around the edges, and wondered if she was mad.

"I suffer from a variety of ugly infirmities, young man. They linger from the plague that beset Dacia. I nearly died of it. I am comfortable here and not stared at. Roderica takes care of my needs and brings me the palace gossip."

Teb stayed with her for some time, telling her lies about Thedria. Whatever she knew of it would likely be from her youth. Countries change. Roderica sat removed from them in a far corner, knitting, looking sour and resentful.

The queen told him Roderica had been with her since the girl was six, and was her only friend. She did not speak of the king again. There was something about the old woman that interested him, something that piqued his curiosity. Maybe she would tell him more if he asked no questions. She seemed uncaring about the affairs of the palace. When he mentioned war, as he described his horses, she seemed to cease to listen, staring down at her wrinkled hands and running one finger along her swollen knuckles. He left her at midmorning, walking back through the dark, windowless halls with Roderica.

"She is lucky to have you for a friend," he said. "She must resent being shut away from palace life."

"She does not resent," Roderica said sullenly. "The queen is of a very even nature." She cast him a hard look, devoid of all the coquettish giggling he had seen at other times. "As for the queen's interest in palace life, *I* bring her all the news she requires."

"And she is never angry at being a prisoner?"

"The queen does not get angry."

"Never?"

"Only if her meals do not suit her. I do the best I can about them. As to the . . . larger issues, the queen's feelings remain removed from them. She does not believe in being . . . emotional."

"I see. And you?"

"What is there to be emotional about? People will

do as they please. Nothing will change them."

His temper flared. He caught himself before he turned on her, biting back his words.

He studied the sharp shadows cast up her face by the lamp she carried. She puzzled him. She seemed a person who followed whatever cause suited her at the moment without any inner commitment—to good or to evil. As if she was little more than a shell.

Maybe the old queen would prove to be much the same, but for some reason he liked her better.

When Roderica left him, turning down her own corridor, he went directly to the stables to see to the tedious training of clumsy soldiers. As he saddled Seastrider he shared with her, in silence, his thoughts about the queen and Roderica. The queen was the more interesting of the two. She was abrupt, had made rude comments about some of the customs of Thedria, and seemed to soften only when he spoke of the talking animals of that land. She caught herself at once, though, and was surly again. Maybe she felt rudeness was a luxury of illness and old age.

He suffered a day of training, taking his three mounted soldiers down the hills toward the city, where they passed loaded wagons of grain bags and stores hidden in linen wrappings. Many wagons unloaded at a long building behind the stadium, and others made their way up the mountain to the palace, to be emptied somewhere behind the inner wall. Food, he supposed. But maybe weapons, too. Interesting that the country had deteriorated so much that it must import food rather than grow what it needed. All the land to the north was open. The farms there lay fallow, fields of crusted brown soil and weeds that could be seen clearly from the palace.

Teb used the sleep song again that night, and the dragons took to the sky like startled birds, not pausing until they were miles out over the sea, away from the palace and all connected with it. Below them lay the small land of Liedref, awash with the aura of dark.

On Liedref they found a young woman gone sour and evil under enchantment of the dark. She had once served the King of Edain as teacher and mistress of his children. He had helped her escape Edain with the children, believing she would keep them safe while he remained behind to battle the invaders. But she was weak, driven by small, greedy envy. The dark found her an easy mark. Soon she was its pawn, caring for nothing but its blood-lust. She murdered three of the king's children and took the other two into slavery.

Even dragon song could not drive the dark from her. Teb fought for her, surrounding her with visions of warmth and caring from her past. But the dark was a mindless force within her. It roared a challenge that pounded in Teb's mind, so his own voice faltered.

The dark won. The host it held was too weak and had embraced its evil too long. In one last, losing effort to free herself, the woman lunged at a dark disciple and stabbed him with his own knife, stood watching his fallen body seep out colorless blood. "I didn't know they could die," she whispered. "I didn't know . . ."

Then she plunged the knife into her own heart, too weak to leave the dark, too filled with its ways to live without it. "I didn't know they could die. . . ."

"They can die," said Teb bitterly, as he held the dying woman. He was able to free the children. The two small girls came sleepily to Seastrider and put their arms around her nose.

All the rest of that night, with the lopsided moon hiding, then showing itself between clouds, Teb and the dragons sang. They freed the minds of the thirty-seven children and two dozen adults, saw consciousness come back to them and the knowledge of who they were. Teb felt their understanding as they were linked once more to their pasts. He felt the excitement of the children as, newly freed, they thought for the first time of real futures chosen without restraint. He felt Seastrider's joy for the children returned from slavery to life. He gave her a hug and mounted. The dragons swept into the wind, racing dawn back to the palace. They dropped down onto the hills as the first gray light touched the sky. They changed quickly, to gallop back toward the stable.

But near to the stables the four horses paused, snorting and staring.

What? Teb said.

Someone hiding in the dark, said Seastrider.

A whole army?

One person.

Well, go on in. What harm can one person do?

The stable was still dark inside. Seastrider approached it warily, the other three crowding close, their ears laid back, their movements tense, ready to strike.

Teb stepped in quietly, filled with fear that someone had seen them in the sky.

Yet it was still very dark. And no one could have beaten them back to the stable. He lit a lamp far down the alleyway. He filled the water and feed buckets, patted Seastrider on the rump, pushed her toward her stall. She turned at once to stare back toward the dark corner near the stable entry. When he approached the corner, she followed him, ready to charge.

"You'd better come out," he said evenly. "I don't like being spied on."

A slim figure stepped out of the blackness. It was Kiri.

She looked at him steadily. Neither spoke. He studied her dark eyes for any hint that she had seen the dragons in the sky, or seen the changing.

Her look was innocent, direct. She glanced past him toward the horses with the same yearning expression he had seen as she stood watching them from the almond grove with her Gram. He liked her thick, straight lashes and the way her brows looked like little wings. She seemed, Teb thought, more like a wild creature than a docile palace page. Watching her steady eyes and the set of her jaw, he wondered that she would take orders at all from the high-handed royal family.

"I came to see the horses."

"I heard you weren't allowed in the stable."

"I'm not. But they're too beautiful for me to stay away. Do you mind? May I speak to them?"

Before he could stop her, she moved past him to Seastrider, who stood with ears back and teeth bared. She laid a hand on the mare's cheek, and Seastrider thrust her ears forward at once, then snuffled at the girl's shoulder, her tail swinging lazily. Teb gaped.

When she went to Nightraider, he blew rollers into her neck, making her laugh, making a first-rate fool of himself. The horses had never acted like that, not with anyone.

"My father was horsemaster for the king, long ago," she said quietly. "Not Sardira. A previous king." Her look was steady. "I used to help him. When King Bayden died, Sardira sent my father away and appointed a new horsemaster. He said I was not to come near the stables. I guess I—" She went silent, her expression going cold as she stared past him toward the stable entry. Teb turned.

Another figure stood in the doorway, etched against the faint dawn light, her skirts swirled around her.

"I guess you made a nuisance of yourself in the stables, little cousin," Accacia said. "I guess you tried too often to tell King Sardira's horsemaster how to run his business." She came across the stable alley holding her skirts up off the earthen floor, though it had recently been swept clean and smooth.

"You should not be here now, Kiri. Sardira would

be interested to know you have disobeyed." Accacia was dressed not for an early-morning ride, it seemed to Teb, but for a formal parade, in a lavender satin riding dress that rippled like water as she moved, shining black boots, and gold circlets binding her bright hair. "I think you had better run along, Kiri. You must not bother the prince. We are off soon on an important ride."

Kiri turned to go, expressionless and straight-backed. "Wait, Kiri," Accacia said. "Perhaps . . ." She looked Kiri up and down. "If you will brush the straw out of your hair and make yourself presentable, you may serve as entourage page. I want four pages. Choose whatever three you like. We leave directly after breakfast." She dismissed Kiri with a flick of her lace cuff.

The horses looked after Kiri eagerly as she left the stable, but when Teb sought in silence for the cause of their warmth toward her, they couldn't tell him. Only that she was, in the sense of their thoughts, one to care about. Their expressions changed completely when Accacia approached them. When she reached to stroke Nightraider's nose he scowled and bit at her, his teeth snapping inches from her face. She backed away, gasping, her hand raised to strike him, then forced a little laugh.

"Oh, they *are* spirited! I love a spirited horse!" She came to Teb quickly and laid a hand on his arm. "Might I ride that wild stallion when we go out this morning? I expect he would not be so challenging once I was on his back, with a proper bit in his mouth and proper spurs."

"We are going out very early," Teb said. "You seem dressed for a grand presentation." He could hardly keep his mind on Accacia for wanting to go after Kiri, for wanting to question her. Kiri was not of the dark; the dragons had proved that. She did not seem to him a shallow person who would have no commitment at all.

"We leave in an hour, Prince Tebmund. I expect you will want to change from your . . . stable clothes." Accacia studied his stained tunic with distaste. "Breakfast is served in the hall. I will have the grooms saddle your mare for you, and the black stallion, along with the rest of the mounts."

"I will saddle my mare," he said softly. "And it would not be wise for you to try any of my horses, princess. They have a strange and cruel dislike of any woman on their back."

"I can handle any horse, Prince Tebmund. I will order a special bridle that—"

"Windcaller bucked off the female horsemaster of Windthorst's western province and the woman was bedridden for six months with a broken hip. Nightraider attacked a visiting woman soldier from Akemada who insisted on riding him and broke her arm with one bite."

Two red splotches flamed across her cheeks. "You are rude, Prince Tebmund. I tell you I can handle your horses."

"I am only trying to protect you. You are far too lovely to be hurt or disfigured by an angry stallion. Come, shall we go to breakfast?"

She stared at him coldly, then swept out ahead of him.

CHAPTER
9

Roderica watched the party depart the stable yard dressed to the teeth, Accacia in her lavender satins, the king's soldiers turned out in full uniform. From her high bedroom window behind the stable she could see them leave the main road and disappear over the crest of the first hill leading down into the city. Such a lot of fuss for a simple ride through the streets. Accacia's idea, she thought, amused. Accacia found the visiting prince more than handsome. Well, let her. He was too involved with those horses to be really interesting. Accacia herself said he was not a very amusing conversationalist at the state meals. All looks and no fun, so why bother? Besides, it was more interesting to watch Accacia make a fool of herself. The queen would be amused at how she overdressed for a simple ride through the city, at how she threw herself at the prince.

Roderica lived as much on gossip as did the shut-in queen, the two of them chewing over other people's lives but not involved in them. Why get tangled in stupid conflicts? Most of the passions that drove folk were pointless, she agreed fully with the queen.

Roderica couldn't figure out what it was lately that made the queen act so strangely. Certainly it was not the secret she carried, at least it had never made her act peculiar before. Roderica had always known the queen's secret, ever since she came to her as a small child. It meant little to her except it *was* a secret to be kept, a degree of loyalty she reserved for the queen alone. Besides, such a condition had no practical use. She watched the last soldiers disappear over the hill. The four foot pages at the head of the procession emerged farther down where the lane rose between ruined buildings. There was a scuffle, as if someone had attacked the pages; then they moved on. Roderica smiled at Accacia's manipulation of little Kiri. How degrading to have to walk on foot, through mud and dung, before a line of mounted royalty and troops.

Accacia had taken Kiri to the stadium games several times, to wait on her where she sat in the royal box. The games always made the child deathly pale. Well, Kiri took such things far too seriously. She'd always had this weakness about animals. The queen had it, too. The old lady was getting worse lately, had taken to talking sentimentally about animals. That was bad enough, but now the queen had begun letting a fox slip into her chambers, thinking she was keeping it secret from Roderica. The dirty little fox came in through a hole in the stone wall that led to an old inner cistern. Roderica had seen it fleeing one night, then later had found its white fur caught on the stone.

She couldn't imagine why the queen would suddenly allow such a thing, a dirty fox slipping in. What could a stupid speaking animal possibly have to say of interest? And why would the queen want to listen? The queen was *her* friend, should want to talk to her, not to a fox. Roderica hadn't much liked Prince Tebmund going there, but at least he was a prince. But a fox— a common animal taking her place as confidant to the queen was quite another matter. Oh, it had been there often. Roderica had no doubt they exchanged confidences, from the look on the queen's face sometimes, smug and secret. Roderica sighed. It wasn't fair that she spend her whole life serving the queen, then be shoved aside for a fox.

She thought of trapping it and presenting it to the king for his stadium games, but that idea made her strangely uncomfortable. Well, she *could* trap it, pay a bargeman to carry the creature across the strait to Ekthuma or Igness—anywhere where it would not return to the queen.

When she left the window to find a suitable box trap, the procession was halfway down the hills into the crowded center of the city.

The royal party moved through the streets with precision, its green uniforms bright, Accacia's lavender satin brighter, the horses clean, sharply groomed, and stepping at a measured pace. Ahead of the double line, the four pages cleared the way of chickens and pigs and small children. Teb watched Kiri, still consumed with curiosity about her.

She walked lightly with a lithe dignity, while the other three pages, all boys, marched with rigid precision, knowing the king's soldiers observed them. Kiri had brushed her green tunic and cap very clean and bound up her hair in a bun at the nape of her neck. She wore her sword with grace, as if used to it. She led the party, on foot, with much more dignity than Accacia showed riding surrounded by soldiers.

They were a party of twenty-six. First came Prince Abisha and a captain of Sardira's army, a broad-waisted man who sat his horse heavily. Then four more captains, two and two—the king had not accompanied them—then Teb and Accacia, and behind them the remaining soldiers. Accacia rode a sorrel gelding that matched exactly her tawny hair, a hard-mouthed horse, as she seemed to require, for she spent a good deal of effort spurring him up into the bit and jerking him, to make him prance. It was all Teb could do not to snatch the reins from those unfeeling hands and give the horse his head. Its neck was already white with foaming sweat, though the other horses were dry. Accacia was looking at the four marching pages with smug satisfaction.

"Sometimes," she said, "people throw things at a royal entourage. It is good to have pages walking in front, to catch the mud and dung. Their swords can drive off troublemakers, too." Then, glancing along the street ahead, she said casually, "Well, I see we have some new beasts of burden. Brought in yesterday's shipping, most likely."

Teb stared at the two blinded, maimed wolves pulling a heavy cart. They were speaking wolves, scarred and thin under the cruel chains, their proud manes cut to a ragged stubble. They walked hesitantly, heads down, blind eyes staring at nothing. Teb was sick with fury and felt Seastrider's revulsion in her rigid walk. Maybe he could find a way to release them, find power to break the chains.

Yet blinded wolves could not survive easily, alone among hostile men. He must wait. He made a silent promise to the pitiful creatures. Soon they passed another speaking wolf, a great male hitched to a wagon of ale barrels. That animal turned his blind face to follow Seastrider's progress, sensing her, sensing Teb, perhaps. Accacia spurred her tired horse into its perpetual prance as, ahead, two men in wrinkled, muddy clothes emerged from a tavern, arguing loudly, walking unsteadily. The pages pushed them aside with the flat of their swords, quick and skilled; the drunks faded into another doorway. The city still dropped toward the sea. To their left a long arm of crowded buildings stretched out along the river, ending at the curved bay tangled with docks and small barges and fishing boats. The wind from the river was heavy with fish and the stink of tanneries.

There were more ruins here from the ancient times,

their stone walls describing generous courtyards, cluttered now with shacks. It had been a graceful city once. Teb saw it in inner vision as it had been long ago. Below the sea cliff, covered now by ocean, had once rolled green, rich hills descending to the Valley of Igness and its orchards and farms, its fields of wheat and rye that had made Dacia wealthy. As the sea had flowed up to cover the land, people had moved up, too, constructing hasty shacks and lean-tos, and digging insufficient drains that were now filled with refuse. The picture was clear in his bard memory, the frantic movement of shops and animals, the confusion, though the sea had risen slowly enough to allow that untidy emigration.

Thakkur, the white otter, had spoken of such things. That was before Teb's bard memory came alive in his mind. Thakkur had stood tall in his cave, his dark eyes filled with ancient knowledge, his voice caught in sadness for the wonders that were all but forgotten. "Humans don't remember . . . the long-shadowed tale of this world, or even that there was a time before the small island countries existed. They don't remember the five huge continents," Thakkur said sadly. They did not remember, Teb thought, the wonders of Tirror before the dark came.

Teb stroked Seastrider's neck, seeing in vision with her the small city nations where each person pursued his own talent in craft or farming, seeing again the wonderful things that were made and grown with the help of the magic Tirror then knew. Seeing the intent bartering and trading as craftsmen traveled from city to city, and children traveled to learn their chosen trades, living with the animals, often, in the old sanctuaries, or with the mining dwarfs in the far mountains. Teb saw how folk's vision of the world, and of themselves, flowed through time, from the very birth of Tirror, all linked in a continuity that had meaning for each person, all kept alive through the song of dragons. The dark had not been strong yet to cast its pall on the world.

Folk did not remember now, as they did then with dragon song, a vision of Tirror's birth. "A ball of gases," Thakkur had said, "formed by a hand of such power that no creature can know its true nature, the power of the Graven Light. But," Thakkur said, "from the very beginning, the fire and bareness and the promise of life lured the dark that always exists in black space. The dark crept through crevices into the molten stone, and it lay dormant. Even the power that made Tirror could not rout it." So the dark had come to the young world, so the dark had waited and grown stronger. It had driven the dragons out at last, and killed or captured the bards. Memory was at last destroyed. Then into Tirror from other worlds came dark beings to join it—came the unliving, came Quazelzeg and his kind.

Ahead, the pages slowed where six men were circled around two women fighting with sticks. The onlookers stared up at the soldiers. The women stopped fighting and stared, too, but no one moved out of the way until the pages drove them back. One staggering man threw up at Kiri's feet. Two more hit out at the pages suddenly, knocking one to the ground, then fled. Pigs wallowed in a mudhole where cobbles had been removed. A little ragged girl came out of a shop carrying a screaming baby and stood staring as they passed. As the pages turned a corner, Kiri glanced back at the entourage. Her eyes met Teb's in an instant of shared disgust; then she looked quickly away.

"It is a city of contrasts," he said diplomatically, when Accacia turned to him. "I thank you for bringing me to see it." He smiled. "Someone has taken the time to grow beautiful roses." He indicated a tiny garden wedged between a cow pen and a closed shop, where a yellow rose vine bloomed.

Accacia sniffed. "Some of them keep flowers—but what is the use of it? They are only peasants. They would do better to grow beans in that space."

It was then, as they turned a corner approaching the harbor, that Teb saw the slave children. A straggling line of ragged children hardly more than babies, carrying heavy bundles on their shoulders, in from the barges at the quay. Five children pulled a wheelless sledge piled with packets of cloth and long bundles that might have held spears. Teb could see chain marks on the children's ankles. He supposed they slept chained at night, as he once had. Tattered tunics covered their backs, likely hiding scars from the lash. He wanted to leap down and cut them loose, and fight whoever would stop him. As he passed close to a line of straining children, he saw the blank, mindless stares that told him the rest of the story.

Beside him Accacia kicked her horse around a pile of barrels and seemed hardly to notice that her gelding nearly trampled three small children struggling with a hamper of clay jugs.

Seastrider had begun to tremble, shivering, so he leaned to rub her neck. She spoke to him with pain, not in words but with the same fury he felt. Seastrider, like every singing dragon, knew clearly all the sins and pain of Tirror's long past. Yet she was driven to fury at the sight of the small slave children.

The four pages stopped at the foot of the cobbled street where it met the quay, and Kiri turned to look back. Their eyes met again for a moment; then he saw Accacia watching, and looked away. If this girl was Accacia's scapegoat, it had not seemed to quell her spirit.

They took a different route returning to the palace, through a nearly abandoned part of the city where a few rag people camped between the broken walls in rooms without roofs. They circled the huge, stone-walled gaming stadium, flanked by a tangle of paintless cottages pushing so close to one another there was no room for animal pens. Accacia had begun a monologue about the intricacies of her family background, to which Teb hardly listened, when suddenly ahead a door opened, and a man with red hair and red beard threw a bucketful of dirty water into the gutter. Teb jerked

Seastrider's halter and stared. *Garit*. It was Garit. He swallowed back a shout and looked away. It was all he could do not to gallop ahead, leap down, and fling his arms around Garit.

Garit stood filling the doorway with his broad shoulders, his red hair and beard like flame, his eyes following the four pages. He hardly looked at Teb as he passed, surely did not recognize him, grown up. Memories flooded back, Garit teaching him to ride when he was five, holding his horse while he mounted, Garit saddling his mother's mare and bringing a newly broken colt for her to ride. Garit's reassuring voice, the night he helped Teb escape from Sivich's army.

Teb leaned down to adjust his boot so he could look back. Garit returned his look seemingly without recognition. Yet was there a spark deep in his eyes? Teb could not be sure.

It had been four years. Teb had been only a child when he escaped from Sivich that night. He had grown, filled out, his face changed maybe more than he guessed. Teb stared ahead, filled with excitement. Garit *was* here in Dacia. Then maybe Camery was, too.

He made note of where he was in the city. When the entourage turned up a side street, Accacia was still talking, as if her pedigree was infinitely fascinating to him.

". . . and her mother was my aunt Rhemia, so of course that makes me cousin to Abisha and in direct line of the throne in my own right, even if I were not to marry him." She stopped speaking long enough to smile. Teb thought her vanity served her in one way. It had helped her retain her own history, even though her view of it was narrow and dull. Prince Abisha, riding ahead, did not turn to look back, though he must have heard her remarks. Accacia prattled on, seemingly unaware of her tastelessness. "That is on my father's side, of course. I lived with my mother's sister after my own parents died—with my aunt and cousin, the little page up there, Kiri. When my aunt died I saw to it, of course, that Kiri . . ."

Teb had ceased to listen and was watching Kiri. She was walking with a tighter gait, as if held by some new tension, as if she wanted to break away running and kept herself steady with effort. As the horses stepped out faster, heading for home, she swung out ahead of them as if relieved.

Had he seen her turn to look at Garit as she passed him? Garit's hand had come up just then to stroke his beard, and Teb's mind had been filled with his presence, so he was really not aware of Kiri.

Now tension filled Teb as the possibilities teased at him. Could there be a connection between them? He thought of the way the dragons responded to Kiri, of seeing her in the candle shop that he thought could be a rebel meeting place. He thought of seeing her return to her cottage late one night, despite the dangers of the city. He watched her striding ahead, his mind filled with possibilities. He meant to find out about Kiri. Just as surely as he meant to return to Garit.

CHAPTER
10

Kiri burned with impatience after Garit signaled her. The slow march back through the city seemed endless. What could be so urgent that he would stand in plain view of the king's entourage the whole time it was passing? The traps the king had set around the city? But she had told him about the traps, and together they had sprung seven and destroyed them. Had they missed one? Had one of the cats been caught? Her heart lurched. Elmmira? But it did no good to imagine such things.

When at last they reached the palace stable, she ducked away from the other pages, into a storeroom beneath the horsemaster's dwelling to wait until the pages had gone on. From the shadows she heard Roderica's voice and Accacia's as the two young women mounted the stairs above her head, probably to comb their hair and repair face coloring in Roderica's room, after sweating in the morning sun.

When they had gone she went quickly through the

palace and servants' quarters, then through the side gate and down to her own cottage, where she changed into rags. Gram forced two oatcakes at her and some hot tea, which she gulped. The old woman's bright eyes questioned, but Kiri could only say, "Garit wants me—I don't know why." She tangled her hair, hugged Gram and kissed the old woman's wrinkled cheek, then was off through narrow back streets toward the core of the city.

Perhaps Garit's urgency had to do with the new child slaves. The children must have been brought by the three new boats that rode in the harbor. The youngsters looked so thin and hopeless. She could imagine what they were fed, and how they slept at night, squeezed together for warmth in their thin garments. The loads they had carried looked far too heavy. Those children would grow up bent in their bodies as well as their spirits, cowed and unresisting. There were the blinded wolves, too. The memory of them sickened her. They were not of Dacia; there had been no speaking wolves in the country for years. These poor animals had come by ship, just as the slave children had.

When she reached Garit's lane just past noon, it was busy and crowded. Three women whispered and laughed as they gathered laundry from fences, half a dozen beggars rummaged in a heap of trash, and on the corner two men argued, swearing, over a stack of cured goat hides. Kiri sauntered like any other street urchin, gawking idly at the arguing men. She began to poke through a pile of trash beside Garit's front step. When no one was looking, she slipped around quickly to the back door. It opened at once, so Garit had been watching through a crack.

One candle burned in the shuttered room. She could smell tea brewing and could smell cat. She saw that in the far corner Mmenimm, the chocolate-colored tom, slept with little crippled Marshy sprawled between his heavy front legs. Marshy's arm was flung around Mmenimm's thick neck, his twisted leg bent at an awkward angle. The shadows of the room took shape; Garit's cot and patched blanket; the wobbly table and two wooden chairs; the iron stove and crowded shelves; Garit's clothes, hung on pegs; a stack of scrappy firewood in the corner. Kiri sat down on the smaller of the two chairs and watched Garit pour out tea into cracked mugs. Everything about the cottage was old and dingy, not because Garit liked it that way, but because anything else would have been hard to come by and would have looked suspicious, as well. He passed her a basket of warm seedcakes that did not match the poverty of the hut. She took two, sipped her tea, and waited, watching Garit over the rim of her cup. He *was* like a great red bull, his flaming hair and beard shaggy, his shoulders broad, his face square, and his nose a bit flat. But his eyes were alive with kindness. She could see anger in his face, now, but something more, as well. She could see a stir of excitement deep down.

"That was a grand parade this morning," he said, scowling. "The king seems bent on impressing this young prince from Thedria."

"It is Accacia who would impress him."

"Oh," he said. "And you saw the lines of new slave children and the captive wolves?"

"Where have they come from? So many small children. And the poor wolves all blinded."

"No, not blind. They only seem to be. A wolf can move very well by scent and hearing."

"And the children?"

"They are slave, all right. They are drugged with cadacus, as well as with the powers of the dark."

"Yes. I saw their faces. What is happening? Why were so many brought here? What do the dark leaders plan?"

"Things are changing, Kiri, and quickly. Something has happened on the far northern islands, something that will affect all our own plans." Garit poured more tea, and she realized she had gulped hers.

He laid a hand on her arm. "The children are from Ekthuma, from Edosta, and even from the dark continent. More will be coming. They were brought with boatloads of arms and supplies—you saw the boats."

She nodded.

"The child slaves will be used to shift the cargo and to wait on the soldiers that will be arriving. Dacia," Garit said evenly, "will be headquarters for raids on more than just Bukla and Edain. Headquarters now suddenly, Kiri, in an attack far greater." His eyes filled with challenge. "Something is happening in the north." He paused, his face alight. "The outer islands, Kiri— the outer islands have rebelled."

She sat staring.

Garit nodded. "Yes—Meron, Wintrel, Liedref. Birrig and Burack. Even Elbon. The outer islands are with us now. The islands of the north are with us."

"But how did it happen? They were so far beyond help. Summer's messages all say—"

"Something has changed the folk of the outer lands. Something has brought them awake, and it has happened only recently." Garit emptied the teapot into her mug and pushed the basket of seedcakes at her.

"It was Summer who brought the news," he said. "She was overheard and nearly captured in Ekthuma, and had to get out fast. She knows something has happened on the outer islands, but she isn't sure what. She is filled with excitement, for whatever it was woke the island folk. They have killed their dark leaders or driven them out. On Wintrel, Yesod and his four consorts were forced over a cliff into the sea."

"Yesod was so powerful. How . . .?"

"The reports were strange and garbled. In Birrig the townsfolk seem to have killed all nine dark leaders. On Liedref the tale is that a woman took the dark leader with her when she killed herself. I don't know how it has happened. It's amazing." Garit's eyes were afire. "The folk of the outer islands have risen. They made their way across the channel three nights ago in heavy seas, sailed and paddled every craft that would float.

"They sacked Lashtel, Kiri. Yes. They burned the city and sent the whole tribe of the unliving—Quazelzeg, too—fleeing back into the interior."

Kiri gaped. "Quazelzeg?"

"Yes. But only because he was unprepared. That won't happen again. I think he had grown complacent with so many victories. He will be twice as vicious now, twice as hard to destroy."

She shivered. It was hard to imagine him as *more* vicious. She wished the rebels had been able to kill him. "I heard nothing in the palace, no messenger, no hint of it."

"I think the dark leaders might not tell this to King Sardira so eagerly. It puts them in a bad light. Sometimes I think Sardira knows a secret that half frightens the dark forces. How else could Dacia have remained neutral so long?"

She was silent for a moment, thinking. "Once," she said, "Accacia told me that the dark would never enslave Dacia. That it could not. Accacia laughed about it."

"What could she have meant?"

"She would say no more. I thought it was one of her exaggerations. But maybe it wasn't. If the dark can't conquer Dacia, and if it is losing to the outer islands . . ."

"No, don't think the dark is on the run everywhere,

Kiri, and certainly not from King Sardira. Summer says they plan to use him, as we have supposed. That soon the dark leaders will converge here to see to the arms and supplies. They mean to attack not only Bukla and Edain but all the outer islands and destroy them, then march on all the continents of this hemisphere. They are livid with anger at this attack. Dacia will be their headquarters. Maybe that's why they let it stay partially free. Perhaps it is more useful that way. Dacia is the central point. With Sardira's cooperative ways, it is the perfect base. This move, now, the sudden arrival of soldiers and supplies in a push for all-out war, is simply much sooner than they planned.

"I saw a runner come down from the palace to investigate the new arrivals, as if the king didn't know they were coming. He went among the ship captains, then returned hastily, this morning at first light. It was not until late last night that *we* knew, when Summer came slipping to my door. She sailed a small boat down from Igness, fleeing Vurbane's troops under darkness. She is sleeping now in the sanctuary, guarded by Elmmira's sisters."

"Is she all right?"

"Only bone tired."

Kiri sighed. "There will be hundreds and hundreds of soldiers besides the dark leaders. How can we win against such an army? There are so few in the city who care, who will join us."

"There is the power of Gardel-Cloor to help us. We will have reinforcements when troops from the outer countries arrive, likely with animals, too. The white fox—the queen's friend," he said, grinning, "has sent word by some of the younger foxes and otters for the animal nations on all the continents to prepare for war." Garit shook his head. "That Hexet. Sometimes I think he knows even more than he tells us. As if he has some secret too personal to trust even to the resistance."

"You don't trust Hexet? Oh, Garit . . ."

"I trust him, Kiri. I get the feeling sometimes that it is a personal confidence. Something that would not affect the war. Or perhaps something he feels it better to deal with alone. Oh, yes, I trust Hexet without reservation. He has led all the stealing parties where the animals have been so successful. They will continue to steal and to sabotage the dark wherever they can. We have excellent supplies of food, thanks to them, and to the stores you located. And we've cleaned out two of Sardira's caches of weapons, hidden them in the usual places, Gardel-Cloor, and the trusted shops . . . you know the places."

She nodded. "And where is Papa?"

"On Ocana with half a dozen others, rallying rebel troops."

She sat quietly. There would be fighting soon. Her father would be in it, Garit, Summer, all of them. The beginning would be like dropping off a cliff with no possible way to turn back.

Garit touched her hand, bringing her back from a

thin edge of fear. "This is not why I wanted you to come. There was another reason."

She waited, watching him, concentrating on how his red beard curled in a shaft of light through the shutters.

"I saw the entourage when you first left the palace this morning, while I was helping the cobbler store arms. I followed you, then raced here through the back streets to have a better look because . . . because I think I know Prince Tebmund. I think that is not his true name."

"And . . . is he not from Thedria? Oh, Garit, not a servant of the dark."

"What do *you* think he is? What do *you* feel?"

She swallowed. "I don't know. I hope he is not of the dark. I trust him, Garit, though I have no reason. He makes me feel . . . a sense of goodness. Almost the way I feel in the palace sometimes for no reason." She shook her head. "There's no sense to it. I'm afraid to trust what I feel."

"It is a sad thing about war, Kiri, that you cannot trust your own instincts."

"But if you know him . . ."

"I may know him. The one I knew was only twelve when I saw him last. One changes a lot from twelve to manhood. He would be sixteen now. If it is he . . ."

"But he saw you, Garit. Have *you* changed so much? If he knows you, wouldn't he have given you some sign? Turned . . . ?"

"If he was careful, he would not. Would you, in this time of war, when even the slightest signal might be noticed by Sardira's soldiers?

"And there might be another reason," Garit said. "I heard once that my friend had lost all memory, didn't even know his name. That he was living on an island with a colony of speaking otters, east of Windthorst, the island of Nightpool. I went there searching for him. He had disappeared, and the otters would tell me little. Their leader was away, traveling on some secret errand . . . at least they were closemouthed about it. Secretive—otters can be damnably secretive. They wouldn't tell me if Tebriel even knew who he was or where he went; they only assured me he wasn't there anymore."

"If he is your friend, Garit—and if he remembers—he will come to you."

"He might be afraid of being followed, of leading Sardira's men here." Garit frowned. "You must find out what you can, Kiri. Learn whether he is Tebriel, son of the King of Auric. Find out if he knows who he is." He paused, watching her. "If he is Tebriel, he is someone urgently important. Someone we need. You are young and pretty. You should have no trouble charming a young man into confiding in you."

"If I had Accacia's charms, maybe."

"Does he seem attracted to Accacia?"

"He was riding with her in that pompous parade. She is very taken with *him*."

"Accacia is taken with everything in pants. If he is who I think, I expect he will have better taste."

"How will I be sure he speaks truly? And how will he know to trust me?"

"If you speak of the tapestries in his palace, that showed the old times and worlds unknown to Tirror. If you speak of his mother wearing a red dress and sitting before the flame tree in her private walled garden. If you speak of his childhood pony, Linnet, who used to want to roll in the river with Teb on his back, and tell him I told you these things, he will know that I trust you, and so can he."

Mmenimm had awakened and was watching them. Kiri knelt beside the great chocolate-colored cat and hugged his muscled neck. He rubbed his tufted cheek against her hair. Marshy did not wake but grasped Mmenimm's leg tighter with one small hand. His breathing was quick and shallow, and she watched the little boy with concern. "He's pale today. He's sick again."

"He has not slept well at night," Mmenimm said. "He sleeps better in the daytime. At night he has strange dreams." The great cat licked Kiri's hand. "Dreams that wake him, feverish with excitement."

Marshy was often white and sick, though at other times wiry and eager. No one could make out what caused the changes. But that he was kin to strange powers, the same as Kiri and Summer, no one doubted.

Marshy woke suddenly, stared up at her, then put

his arms up sleepily. She gathered him in. His little body felt cold, except where he had been pressed against Mmenimm.

"I dreamed, Kiri." He stared up at her, his blue eyes swimmy from sleep. "I dreamed of dragons. In the sky—all in the sky and the wind . . ."

She pressed her face to him and felt the pain he felt, and knew how hopeless such dreams were. "I know, Marshy. I know. I dream of dragons, too."

He reared back with surprising strength and stared at her. "No, Kiri. This was real—a real dream. They are there. Dragons . . ."He stared at her boldly, crossly. "In the sky, Kiri! They are there in the sky!"

She pressed his face gently against her shoulder, hugging him, and exchanged a look with Mmenimm and with Garit, sat rocking Marshy for a few moments, then laid him back in the shelter of Mmenimm's warm paws. She felt sick with her own hopeless longing, stirred by Marshy's innocent dreams. There were no dragons anymore. They had no right to dream of dragons; neither of them had. It only made them miserable.

She left the cottage soon afterward.

A block from her doorway she saw soldiers on the high road coming from the north. Not Sardira's green-clad troops, but soldiers uniformed in the garish yellow of the dark forces and led by drummers beating a slow dirge that chilled her through. They had come by barge from the north, from the dark huge continent of Aquervell, there could be no doubt. She slipped up between

114

houses and onto a tile roof where she could watch undisturbed.

Forty horsemen, two by two, entered the palace keep that led to the stables. The eight riders at the head of the battalion sat their horses stiffly and did not look to left or right. Their hands on the reins never moved. Their faces above the yellow tunics were cold and sallow. Kiri swallowed back gall and wanted to turn and run from them, as far away as she could.

Instead of running, she went quickly through back ways to the rear of the stable beneath the horsemaster's apartments. She slipped in between two haystacks directly behind the stalls, where she could listen unseen, stood pressed against the prickly hay trying to hear over the pounding of her own heart.

CHAPTER
11

Teb burned to get to Garit. The return ride up to the palace seemed to take forever. He thought of pretending Seastrider was lame or sick and falling back, riding back alone. But there were too many eyes to see him. If not the soldiers, then those within the city itself. Seastrider began to sweat lightly. Accacia swatted at flies buzzing in the heat and prattled endlessly. When they reached the stable at last, Accacia insisted on waiting for Teb while he groomed Seastrider, so she could walk with him to the late lunch she had planned. She stood well out of the way as he rubbed the white mare down.

"I should think you would leave such work to the grooms."

He ignored her, took his time with the grooming ritual, hot towels, rubdown, brushing, all of it, as he tried to invent a way to escape her without causing suspicion, and get down into the city.

You had best wait, Tebriel. She watches you too closely.

I must see Garit. It's why we came here—partly why.

We will go tonight, wait until tonight.

He worked for some time, slowly, making Accacia wait. Then suddenly Seastrider began to fidget and paw.

What's the matter with you?

She turned her head to stare at him. *Can't you sense it? Someone—a speaking animal, Tebriel. Nearby.*

Well, I suppose so. In the city—

No. Her ears twitched eagerly. *Here, in the palace itself.*

Stop twitching your ears; Accacia is staring. What animal? Why would a speaking animal come to the palace?

I don't . . . A fox, Tebriel! Yes. A kit fox.

Can you tell where? Can you tell what it's doing?

No. Only . . . She stood staring into emptiness for a moment. *Only that it comes to . . . to see a friend, I think.* Seastrider snorted and shook her mane. *It comes secretly, Tebriel. By a secret way.*

"Are you nearly finished?" Accacia said. "They will have let the lunch get cold. Or burnt."

He went at last, following Accacia, his mind teeming with curiosity about the fox, and still filled with a pounding eagerness to find Garit. On top of these thoughts remained a stubborn picture of Kiri

117

turned back at him, her dark eyes filled with knowing.

The fox sat before the queen waiting for her to wake, giving little panting huffs to make her stir. It was noontime, but this room was always filled with thick night. The lamp burned softly, sending a glow across his silver-white coat. His tail was bright white, bushy, and there was a dark gray streak across one shoulder where a knife wound had healed. His eyes were dark and intelligent, his alert ears thrust forward. He watched the queen sleeping with her mouth open, said, "Huff," again irritably, then in exasperation he gave one muffled, sharp bark, glancing uneasily at the locked door. The queen opened her pale eyes, staring at him blankly, then smiled, so all her wrinkles deepened. She sat up in bed and tried to straighten the covers so he would have a warm place to sit.

He jumped up when she beckoned, pawed at the tangle of blanket she had arranged for him, then sat very straight and regally, regarding her with half amusement and half irritation. He could never be truly angry with her, but there were times she tried his patience.

"Did you tell someone about me?" he asked. "Did you tell Roderica? There was a trap in the passage tonight."

"Oh . . ." Her hand flew to her mouth. "What kind of trap? Not . . ."

"No, not a killer trap. A box trap—but just as

confining, Queen Stephana. Who . . . ?"

"I told no one. You know I wouldn't. Oh, that terrible girl, she has been spying on us! Wait until I catch her, I will flail her."

"With a whip?" he asked, hiding a smile.

"With words, of course. It's all I have. Oh, please . . . you weren't hurt?"

"Of course not. I sprang it easily, then fixed it so she can't use it again. Of course, she will bring others."

"Not when I'm through with her." The queen looked completely undone. The fox thought it was the first time he had ever seen her truly concerned about something. He was touched and flattered. He settled down more comfortably on the nest of blankets, prepared again to try to change the queen's stubborn mind.

He was Hexet, originally of the island of Kipa in the Benaynne Archipelago. He had escaped the island during Quazelzeg's early raids. Hundreds of animals, and some humans with them, had swum the straits to Bukla and Edain and Dacia as Quazelzeg's shipborne soldiers sacked the islands.

Some folk had gone back, and a group of animals and men had retaken a few of the islands. But it was a never-ending battle to keep the dark raiders out, successful mainly because Quazelzeg's forces were now more urgently occupied on larger lands. The small islands of the archipelago had little to offer. They had never been heavily populated. Hexet, with a handful of others, had come to settle on the rocky, barren southerly tip of Dacia, hoping to help the resistance movements that were growing among the animals. He had once been a leader of many foxes and was known as Hexet the Thief. His small band had been constantly at work for some five months, stealing food stores from the palace and ferrying them, with the help of a few otters, around the tip of Dacia to the sanctuary of Gardel-Cloor, for emergency supplies. War would come, rebellion would come, but this war would not be lost through siege and starvation. It was one of the otters who had told Hexet about the captive queen. Curious, Hexet had found a way in to her. He had been coming ever since. He sat up now, studying her old, wrinkled face, seeing the defiance there. She knew very well what he meant to say. He sat as straight and tall as he could manage and fixed her with a look of authority.

She stared back at him, her own demeanor powerful in spite of her ragged, unkempt condition, in spite of her illness and weakness. A reminder of her true nature looked out for that instant, queenly and austere. "Can we not just talk? Can you not simply tell me tales of the fox nation? Do we have to go through this argument every time?"

"We would not have to argue at all if you would be reasonable."

"Or if you would be civil and remember your manners. One does not defy a queen."

"I defy you," he said softly, his dark eyes gleaming and his sharp teeth showing in a quick snarl. "We *must* join together, all of us must, if we are to save Tirror."

"I can save nothing. I am a sick, helpless old

woman and I want only to be left alone."

"You could save more than you know. If you would try. If you cared."

"I can do nothing. I am alone; those skills are dead and would be of no use anyway without— No one can fight alone."

"You are not alone. The hostages from Merviden have risen, Queen Stephana. They have retaken two cities. The underground forces move strongly in the nations of the Nasden Confederacy. You could help them if you cared. You could help Dacia. You still have power; you know you do. Though it may not be as strong as it once was.

"My brothers work with the rebels, Queen Stephana. The foxes, the otters and wolves, and the great cats. Many of us have died. You could help us. You could save many." He knew her weakness. He moved forward over the tangle of blankets, put aside his dignity, and lay down with his head in her lap. As she stroked his lush silvery coat, her face softened. She touched the soft white fur under his chin with one finger.

"They have died," he said. "Many foxes have died slowly, in pain, the same as human children have died."

He stayed a long time, letting her stroke him, telling her of atrocities to humans and animals—though it was the pain of the animals that touched her. She had long ago put away from herself much empathy for humankind—as if the world of humans as she knew

it, the king perhaps, had betrayed her beyond re-
deeming. He left in a flash when he heard Roderica's
key in the door, then waited far down the passage in
darkness.

Roderica discovered the trap and shouted out with
fury before she remembered herself and withdrew into
a protective calm. She didn't care. It didn't make any
difference; she didn't want to fuss around with a dirty
fox, anyway. She listened to the queen's scolding without emotion, agreed with her that she had done a bad
thing, said she wouldn't do it again. Afterward she
went on up to the small dining chamber feeling tired
and dull. Accacia's entourage had returned. Accacia
was waiting for her, tapping her foot. Prince Tebmund
and Prince Abisha stood talking together in a corner.
Roderica had passed the newly arrived captains from
the north as they entered the larger dining hall to take
private lunch with the king.

Roderica suffered through lunch in silence, hating
foxes, hating that fox who so charmed the queen and
who had caused her scolding. When the tedious meal
was finished, she watched Accacia lead Prince Tebmund off on a tour of the palace—whether to keep
him out of the way of the visiting army, or because
Accacia was still intent on romance, Roderica didn't
know or care.

"We will go up to the high wall first," Accacia said
softly. Her satin dress caught the light of the banked

candles as they left the small dining chamber. "It's cool there with the sea wind, for it's nearly on top of the palace." She ushered him into a dark passage. He followed her swinging light uneasily, wishing he had found a satisfactory way of evading her after lunch. But Seastrider was right; it was best to wait until nighttime to go to Garit. Accacia prattled on, thrusting her lamp into open galleries to pick out black spaces and towering furniture, telling him which were meeting rooms, which the chambers of the palace guards and retinue, all seemingly open for inspection. She made wry comments about the palace residents, and glided so close to him that he felt quite warm and uncomfortable. Her voice was too insinuating and personal. Her relationship with Prince Abisha puzzled him. They were to be wed, but she flirted with everyone. Maybe Abisha didn't have the courage to alter her ways.

The looks between Accacia and the king left more questions unanswered.

The black passages opened occasionally in a tall, narrow window shockingly bright with sun. Each one showed them to be higher up the mountain into which the palace was carved. Suddenly at a turn in the passage Teb felt a sharp sense of evil. It lingered for some time, perhaps an aura of evil from the dark leaders dining in the hall below. Then, as they approached an ironclad door, a feeling so powerful struck him that he stopped, staring at the crossed iron strips that bound the oak, his hands trembling. A feeling of powerful magic, of brightness, of infinite goodness.

He felt his pulse pounding; he wanted to see inside. He must find the source of this power.

"The king's treasure rooms," Accacia said casually, though she was looking at him with curiosity. "I do not have a key, Prince Tebmund. Are you so interested in Sardira's treasure as to stand staring, your face gone white?"

"It . . . is the door," he lied. "The pattern of crossed strapping on the door reminded me of something, another door. It stirred unhappy memories, of someone who died," he said, pleased with his inventiveness. He took her hand. "Come, let's find the top of this grand maze, so we can have a real view of the city."

The sense of goodness followed him strongly as they moved up the black stone passages to a flight of narrow steps. At the top of these, they faced a tall arch filled with sky. Beyond was an open walkway, where they stood looking down upon the city, the wind tugging at them.

She moved close to him. "The view pleases you, Prince Tebmund?"

"It is magnificent." But his mind was on the treasure room.

She touched his cheek. He ignored her, studying the city laid out below, seeing it clearly now in daylight where, from the sky, it had been too dark. He could see the route they had taken that morning. He tried to see the ruined tower near Garit's cottage. Accacia pressed her shoulder against him, clasping her arms around herself in the chill wind.

"How long have you lived in the palace?" he asked absently, wishing she would keep her distance.

"Always. Didn't I tell you that? My father was a captain to the king. He died in battle, but my uncle was horsemaster, so, of course, I stayed. Then—" She brushed a fleck of dust from his sleeve and looked up at him openly.

"I was Sardira's mistress, before his dying wife made such a fuss. I've never understood that. The king moved me to the west tower and promised me to Abisha. He promised *her* he would not take another queen, though she is bedridden and useless." Accacia sighed. "What power she has over him, to make him adhere to such a promise, I cannot really say. Why should she be so selfish? She has lived past her time. She talks of dying but she does not intend to do it."

Teb turned away, shocked and angry at her rudeness. Maybe she had had more wine at the noon meal than he noticed. A flock of small brown birds came tumbling in the wind, nearly into their faces. Teb swallowed his anger and smiled down at her. If she was feeling her wine, he would not waste a good opportunity. Already her guide to the location of various guards' quarters had been worthwhile and could prove useful. Information about the queen might be very useful indeed.

"The old queen must be a tyrant," he said lightly.

"She's a bitter old woman who weaves her days around palace gossip, and is a burden to the king."

"And is the crippling she suffers a painful one?"

"Oh, yes," Accacia said casually. "She should have been dead long ago."

"She makes life difficult for you?"

"Not particularly. I make my own life." She gave him a slow, warming look and drew her hand softly down his cheek.

He took her wrists gently and held them. "I would not distress Prince Abisha by making light with his betrothed," he said coolly.

"It would be difficult to distress Abisha. He cares nothing for me." At his surprised look, she smiled. "Most royal marriages are made for convenience, Prince Tebmund. Is it not so in your country?"

"My parents married for love. Perhaps I am old-fashioned in thinking that even a royal marriage should be so."

"Unrealistic would describe your view more exactly." She turned away and started along the narrow stone balcony that wrapped itself around the juttings of the mountain, lost to view ahead of them. They walked slowly, the lamp's flame faded to a transparent ghost in the sunlight. Teb felt Accacia's stubborn desire for him as strong as the eastern wind that pushed up from the sea. Deliberately he turned his mind from her. They did not speak again until they began to descend, when she took his hand.

"The leaders from Aquervell will be at the supper table tonight, Prince Tebmund."

"Supper should be an elegant affair." He assumed all the private discussion would have been finished by suppertime. He would give a lot to hear those conversations. "Are the Aquervell captains frequent visitors to Dacia?"

"They come fairly often. They enjoy the . . . pleasures of the city."

Pleasures, he thought with disgust. He was sure the un-men enjoyed them. Their presence here would make things difficult. He hoped he and the dragons had enough power to shield themselves from discovery. The dark would come down with everything it had if it discovered the truth.

Maybe he should send the dragons away at once, go by himself into the city to Garit, disguise himself and work with the resistance from there.

Yet if the unliving did sense him and follow him, he would lead them straight to Garit. He had better face the dark leaders head-on. Do it boldly, and at once.

What he meant to do *was* bold, and dangerous. The dark would be closer to the dragons than it had ever been.

He knew from Seastrider how strong the shapeshifting power had grown. The dragons had reluctantly agreed to suffer the indignity of being touched and ridden by the unliving, if they must. He knew also that with increased shape-shifting power, danger increased: The shape-shifter might not be able to return to his true form. The very magic that held the shape steady even in the face of dark forces could well freeze the dragons into their alien shapes permanently.

Yet if he did not offer the use of the horses to the dark leaders, they would demand it. It was better to offer and keep the upper hand. This experience would not come easily for the dragons, would be painful and unnerving for them.

"How long will the leaders from the north be staying?" he asked, watching her. "Perhaps they would like to try my horses . . . learn their special fighting skills."

"I think the king mentioned it to them. I suppose there would be buyers among them."

They descended the south parapet with Accacia walking close, her honeyed scent heavy around him. He left her at the north tower stair, pleased with the bits of information he had gleaned, annoyed he had not gotten more. He went quickly toward the stables with a sudden sense of unease, a sudden turmoil of fury that was not his own.

He found the four horses sweating in their open stalls, their retreat blocked by a ring of yellow-uniformed soldiers. A captain of the dark was trying to put a halter on Starpounder. Teb heard the black stallion scream, found him rearing and striking at the heavy-shouldered captain, his fury so great Teb could already see a faint dragon-image ready to surface. He raised his hand and shouted. Starpounder paused rearing, came down to strike his front hooves inches from the captain's head, his teeth bared, his eyes burning with a wildness that no true horse could match.

The captain did not step back. His face was frozen into a sallow mask of contempt.

CHAPTER

12

The un-man was no taller than Teb, but broader and heavier, with shoulders humped forward, drawing a line of wrinkles across his yellow tunic. He took Teb's measure with flat gray eyes, then turned back to face Starpounder. The stallion's face, with lips drawn back, was pulled into a killer's smile. His body was poised ready to strike again. When the captain thrust the halter at his head, Starpounder exploded, rearing, striking. Teb shouted and grabbed him—he came to the ground and backed off, but still he was tensed like a spring, pressing against Teb, glowering at the un-man.

"Get away from him, Captain. You cannot halter him; no one can unless you know the signals."

The captain's voice was as flat and expressionless as his eyes. "Then show me the signals. How do you expect to sell creatures that will not obey and submit?"

"The stallion will obey the man to whom he is sold. I will teach the signals to that man."

"Show them to me. Now."

"When you have purchased and paid for the animal, I will do so."

The un-man's fury was like the silent lash of a whip. "Do you know who I am?"

"You are a captain of the army of Aquervell, and so captain to Quazelzeg."

"I am High Captain Leskrank. I am captain to Supreme Ruler Quazelzeg, and to General Vurbane, ruler of Ekthuma, as well. I serve them on special mission. I desire to ride this stallion."

"I will be most happy to oblige," Teb said, controlling his anger. "But *I* will halter and saddle him." *Be still, Starpounder. You agreed to it; now swallow your fury and bear it.*

Starpounder glowered at Teb, snorting, ears back, then came to him reluctantly. He put his head into the halter Teb held, but Teb could feel the effort it took. Teb stroked the stallion until at last he felt the fury of the dragon subside and calm. He saddled Starpounder with Leskrank's own black war saddle, the sword still dangling at its side. He tightened the girth and gave the halter reins to the heavy-shouldered, gray-faced leader. Leskrank stared at the thin halter but evidently had been told, perhaps by Sardira, that was all Teb allowed on the horses.

"You must remove your spurs first," Teb said. "He will not tolerate spurs."

The man gave Teb a cold stare. "I am used to being master of my mounts. This stallion will learn that, when he belongs to me." He moved to mount. Star-pounder backed away and would not let the captain near him. Leskrank jerked the halter strap, but that did not faze Starpounder.

"When you remove your spurs," Teb said, "he will let you mount docilely."

Leskrank did so at last, and Starpounder came forward to stand still as the heavy captain mounted. Teb could feel the tension of the other three horses, could see the dragonfire behind their eyes. He slipped Sea-strider's halter on and swung onto her back, to ride beside Captain Leskrank. The other soldiers drew back from Windcaller and Nightraider, who stood eyeing them with challenge.

On the broad grass practice field, Sardira's soldiers drew back so the two riders had the flat meadow to themselves. Teb showed Leskrank the special signals that he had taught to Sardira's soldiers, signals he and the dragons had agreed on before they came to Dacia. Leskrank trotted Starpounder in circles, galloped him, then began to practice the signals.

On command, Starpounder reared to strike as in battle, spun so fast the heavy captain was nearly un-seated, ducked to right, then to left, under the attack of Teb's own sword in mock battle, spun again, backed, and, in a surprising launch of inventiveness, in a ma-neuver they had not worked out together, reared over Seastrider and snatched the blunt side of Teb's blade in his teeth and wheeled away bearing the weapon. Any other soldier would have laughed with pleasure.

Leskrank's expression did not change, except that his eyes burned with the desire to own this beast.

"I am working on signals for that maneuver and others," Teb told Leskrank as they walked the horses back toward the stables. "I will be happy to have you put the stallion through his new paces, once they are perfected." If we are here, he thought. For now they had another reason to vanish quickly from the palace, before the dark leaders tried to buy or steal the four horses.

But Leskrank made no offer of purchase. While Teb was sponging off the horses in the stable yard, the dark captain went off toward the main hall with no offer, no word, no change of expression. Teb squeezed out the sponge and looked after him. Leskrank's men followed him in silence, until at last Teb and the four were alone.

He does not mean to buy us, Seastrider said. *Why should he? I can see it in his face. He means simply to take us. He means to teach his soldiers the signals, then ride off on us when he returns to the dark continent. He would make a bitter meal, but I would relish feeling him writhe in my jaws.*

Roasted first by dragon fire, Starpounder said, *and even so, he would not be palatable. Of course, he means to kill you, Tebriel, if you try to stop him.*

Teb smiled, imagining the four horses turning suddenly to dragons and finishing off Leskrank and his troops.

He will do nothing, Seastrider said, *until he is sure*

he has learned all the signals and your methods of training. Until he understands how to make us submit to his will. She shook her mane and snorted. *The unliving may detest knowledge and skill, Tebriel. But when a skill is useful to them, they mean to have it.*

Teb stayed with the horses for some time, stroking and grooming them, for the presence of the dark had left them all edgy. Starpounder, having resisted his urge to kill the un-man, was sweating and fidgeting now and could not settle. Suddenly, as Teb brushed him, his body became translucent, black-gleaming scales showing through. They all stood frozen as Starpounder brought the force of the shape-shifting under control, subsiding at last into the stallion's satin curves.

Seastrider did not lose her image, but she pawed and shook her head, and nipped at the flesh on her shoulder. Teb did not know how much longer they dare stay here, with the dragons' patience wearing so thin.

We will conserve our power, Tebriel. We will practice patience, all of us will, Seastrider said, glowering at Starpounder.

But it would not be long after the state supper that night that Seastrider, too, found her powers changed, and in a different way.

Teb didn't look forward to supper. He dressed carefully, swallowing his disgust at having to dine with the unliving and their amoral followers.

Sometimes he thought he hated the human men who served the dark more than he hated the unliving. The unliving were patterned by their own unchangeable evil natures. They were formed of evil and could not choose any other way.

Human men could choose. Sivich, who had murdered his father, had had a choice. He had chosen deceit. He had served the King of Auric for years before he turned on him, and on Teb and Camery and the soldiers loyal to the king.

Teb descended the west tower and went along through several huge rooms to the state dining hall, where the royal party was standing before a windowed alcove, taking mithnon, awaiting the entrance of the king. Accacia was robed in a clinging apricot gown that complemented the yellow tunics of the dark captains. All seven captains were there, all un-men. Their six lieutenants were human men, but sallow and cold-looking. General Vurbane, the last of the group of eight unmen, arrived with King Sardira, who, robed in his perpetual black, a black velvet tunic topped by a black fur cape, stood out sharply against the bright colors. The king took only one glass of mithnon, then was seated in his tall, black chair at the head of the table.

The purple-and-amethyst table setting was set off with oil lamps that burned with violet flame, making the faces of the eight leaders of the dark armies even more grayed and deathlike. Their voices were dry and expressionless. Surrounded by the eight unliving, Teb was gripped by a cold fear.

He had been too angry, at the stable, to try a power

of shielding against the un-man. Now he tried, with a heated urgency, and felt the strength of the dragons helping him. Leskrank had been the only one he faced at the stable. Now there were eight of the unliving watching him, with time to observe him carefully.

General Vurbane was seated directly across from Teb, next to Abisha, close enough so Accacia, next to Teb, could ply her charms on him. Teb found it strange to see an un-man who had been badly wounded, for he thought of them as nearly invulnerable. He knew they could die, though their blood did not run red but pale like mucus, and if there was a dark inner self to escape the dying body, it was not like a human soul. Yet even having himself seen them injured and dying, he never got used to it, so strongly did his mind cling to the idea of their invincible power. Vurbane had suffered a wound that left the right side of his face rippled in a wide scar from chin to hairline, ending in a ragged bald spot. The tip of his smallest right finger was missing. His eyes were icy, his lips thin and straight.

Captain Leskrank was seated across the table to Teb's left, where he could watch Teb and could flirt with Accacia. She played round robin with all the men near her, ignoring Abisha and the few women seated close by. She excited rivalry skillfully, thriving on it. General Vurbane seemed well aware of her style, accepting her favors as if he had a right to them. Abisha watched the two of them, visibly irritated. He had been drinking heavily, and soon his sullen voice rose above the rest, sarcastic and baiting. "I understand, General, you unearthed a spy in your palace. I am told the girl escaped you."

Vurbane glowered, his scarred face drawn tight.

"She must have been clever," Abisha said smugly, "to have eluded all your fine soldiers."

As Vurbane turned, his scar reflected the lavender light, casting his face into a mask of horror that chilled Teb. "The girl was clever, I suppose, for her kind. A mere accident that she escaped. We will find her."

"A pity, though. Had she served you long?"

"She served my household for two years," Vurbane said stiffly. "She seemed a docile creature, but who knows, with humans." He looked Abisha over, seeming to warm to his subject. "The girl was extremely young. One of those pale, blond types . . . tall and well turned out," he said, leering. "But she was, like all humans, sly and tricky."

Abisha reddened. Vurbane continued, "She was seen clearly talking to a known spy in the marketplace. Their conversation was reported; guards were sent at once to arrest her."

"But she escaped them all," Abisha said, ignoring Vurbane's insults.

Vurbane looked at him coldly, the purple light flaring along the side of his face. "My troops are quite competent, Prince Abisha. It was a wild fluke that she escaped—disappeared before they arrived."

Abisha signaled for more wine and sat back heavily

in his chair, observing Vurbane. "Maybe someone warned her—another spy. You are right, General Vurbane, such people are . . . a menace."

Vurbane's words echoed in Teb's mind, *One of those pale, blond types . . . young . . .*

"We do not know," Vurbane said, "how the girl was warned—*if* she was. But we will find out," he said coldly. "There was a wild story about some huge owl swooping down over the market moments before the troops arrived. My slow-witted peasants believed it alerted her—laughable, what the ignorant believe."

Teb ate slowly, tasting nothing. Could it be Camery? Pale, blond . . . young . . . and on the island where Nightraider had sensed someone. And the owl . . .

It was the big owl, Red Unat, who had brought word that Camery was gone from the prison tower in Auric. Red Unat worked with the resistance, had given his whole commitment to tracking the dark. Teb's thoughts were cut short by Nightraider's silent voice.

She is my bard. I still do not sense her, but if she is there—I will search Ekthuma for her.

Teb sensed the cold wind as the black dragon leaped skyward.

I will search for her. . . .

Nightraider was gone.

"We closed off the five crossings," Vurbane was saying, "and kept watch for several days. We turned out the cottages and shacks, searched thoroughly, but no sign of the wench." Vurbane touched his scar. "She

138

could not have escaped Ekthuma, unless she swam to her death in the sea.

"Very likely," he said, smiling, "she took her own life in one way or another. Her kind will do that." His eyes gleamed. "We will find her body eventually. Unless the sharks ate her."

His purple-tinged smile and glinting eyes sickened Teb.

"Suicide," Vurbane said, tasting the word, savoring it. "It is interesting to watch suicide. It sometimes has amusing results. Such panic, such commitment and dedication, to—what? Why do they fight so hard, these dedicated peasants? There was a crone, a rag woman on Cayub who threw herself into the sea when my troops overtook her, impaled herself on a spiked rock and lived three days gasping for help. The troops waited to see her die." He licked his lips. "Then that tin vendor that set himself afire—and afforded my soldiers an unexpected and interesting entertainment. Unfortunately, I missed it. There are too few such diversions," he said pleasantly, "in these dull times. That is why, my dear Sardira, we like so much to make these refreshing visits to Dacia. Now tell me, what is the nature of the contestants for tomorrow's stadium games? And what nature of . . . other entertainment have you provided? We have been limited in our pleasures far too long, training on that cursed rock island off Ocana, at the ends of nowhere."

"We have some new young slaves," King Sardira

139

said. "Boys *and* girls." His robed figure in the huge carved chair was a pool of blackness at the head of the table. His thin lined face seemed now, in comparison with the gray pallor of the eight unliving, really very healthy and alive. His suggestion of the use of boys and girls disgusted Teb.

"There are a few horses ready to be put down," the king said. "We might bring out some of my guard lizards from the vaults; their teeth are excellently sharp. We have the blind wolves you shipped to us from Aquervell, of course. Ah, and we have captured some of those cursed speaking cats, my dear Vurbane. They're fighters, all right, and should make good sport, pitted against anything of your choice. Too bad we don't have your little escapee to run in with them. We will drug the bulls with cadacus; it makes them crazy. They will make excellent sport with those cats clawing in panic for their lives."

Teb listened with revulsion. The capture of any animal tore him with rage, but that speaking animals would be tortured made his fury rise so it was all he could do not to leap up and beat the king to a pulp. He held himself rigid until his temper eased under control.

He meant to release those cats.

Yet he could sacrifice much if he failed. He was very close now to learning something that could be vital. He must find the source of bright magic in the locked treasure chamber. He must not be captured before he did.

He felt sure Accacia knew what that magic was, and

140

when supper was at last finished, he maneuvered her away while the officers were rising and Vurbane had gone up to speak privately with the king. He gave Accacia a smile. "Will you show me a little more of the palace before you join the general and his captains?"

She glanced toward Vurbane, saw him and the king deep in conversation, then took Teb's arm. "Perhaps a short walk, Prince Tebmund."

She led him up a side stair to an upper landing that overlooked the dining hall, then out along the parapet as before, but in the opposite direction. They descended a second, winding flight. "There are terraces here, Prince Tebmund, between the chambers and the wall of the mountain. I have a favorite."

They came to a gate of iron wrought into the shapes of branches and leaves, then into the closed terrace it sheltered, a small, dark garden lit by seven candle lamps, walled by the mountain at the back and planted with damp ferns and twisting vines. It was chill and dismal, with only a thin view of the stars. The palace wall that edged the garden was black stone, carved into pierced patterns. There was no sense of either good or evil, only of isolation. She pulled him down onto the black bench, brushing a leaf away.

"This is pleasant, Prince Tebmund." Her eyes were warm, soft, in the candlelight. "I find you very compatible—to walk with, to be with. Far more so," she said, "than even General Vurbane."

"You seem comfortable with him. And with all the northern leaders."

"They . . . are necessary," she said candidly. Perhaps she had seen his own distaste at supper. "And they pass the time pleasantly. What else is there to do in life but pass the time as pleasantly as you can?"

"I would have thought you would pass the time with Prince Abisha."

"I told you he cares nothing for me. It was Sardira who decreed that we wed."

"And, of course, it is Sardira to whom you owe allegiance."

"We all owe allegiance to the king."

She wasn't so open, now, about her personal life. It was going to be harder to get her to speak freely. He watched her appraisingly, then put his arm around her and tried to weave soft thoughts, bringing power around her. He must work slowly, not ask questions too soon.

"I imagine," he said lightly, "that you and the king find the northern leaders exciting companions at the stadium games, appreciative guests." He felt her tension, but she was beginning to relax under his power; her eyes were softer, her body giving gently against him. "I expect they are, themselves, a rather exciting game."

"All life is a game," she said dreamily. "What else would it be?" She cuddled sleepily against him.

"A game with the dark," he said, prompting her. "An exciting game, Accacia."

There was a flash of awareness, then her hands went limp and the last touch of brittleness left her.

"A game with the dark . . . for what stakes?" he said.

It took all his strength of mind to force her will to his, but at last she said softly, "Big stakes, perhaps. If we play their game, give them all they want, we get along very well. . . ."

"What do they want, Accacia? Pleasure, of course. Pleasure . . ."

"Yes, pleasure." She seemed vaguer now. He must not let her grow disoriented. "And Dacia is . . ." Her voice drifted off. She was too dreamy. He forced her awake.

"Dacia is . . ." he prompted.

"Dacia is . . . the center. The city's favors—women, drugs, and the gambling of the stadium games . . ."

"And the center for what else?"

"For weapons, supplies, for a war base . . ."

"And they intend . . . ?"

"To conquer all Tirror, of course. Except . . . except Dacia."

"Why is that, Accacia? Why will they leave Dacia free?"

She stirred against him and sat up straighter, but still she was docile to his will. She looked at him softly, waiting. He took her hands in his.

"How do you know," he asked gently, "that the dark leaders won't enslave Dacia with the rest of Tirror . . . when Dacia is no longer of use to them?"

Her look shuttered suddenly. He pressed his thought

143

stronger until she relaxed. He let his lips brush her cheek.

"How do you know they won't enslave Dacia?"

"They cannot," she said dreamily.

"And why is that?"

"There is a powerful talisman in the palace. It prevents them from subduing Dacia." She snuggled into his shoulder. He strained to hold the spell.

"What power, Accacia? What power could be so strong?"

Suddenly she straightened, pulled away, staring at him with confusion, then with fear.

13

Accacia rose angrily and began to pace the dark garden. The seven candles flickered at her passing. Teb did not release the effort of his spell but sought to bring her back into it. When at last she turned, her eyes again held a hint of sleepiness. She spoke uncertainly.

"What knowledge . . . do you seek, Prince Tebmund?" She seemed to be trying to remember his exact words, as if all she could bring to mind was the power in which he had held her.

What had broken that power?

He brought all the force he could; he felt the dragons helping him.

"I seek only to understand."

He was sweating, his body too tense, his mind torn with haste. The dark leaders would wonder, if they were gone too long. They could come searching.

Unless they *knew*. Unless it was *their* power that had warned her. He felt the forces of dark and light battle around him on a scale he could barely comprehend. As he brought the dragon magic around Accacia, shadows stirred across her still figure. She came slowly to the bench and sat beside him. He took her hands, drew her close.

"Trust me, Accacia. Tell me now . . . what talisman protects the palace of Dacia?" Her hands were warm within his, relaxed. "What difference would it make if you tell me? What harm . . . ?"

"What difference . . . ?" She sighed.

"What talisman prevents the dark from enslaving Dacia? What power so strong . . . ?"

"The power . . ." She studied their clasped hands as if puzzling over her own thoughts. "The power of the dragon," she said heavily.

He stared, his blood racing. *The dragon . . .*

"The power of the dragon's lyre . . ."

His pulse had quickened unbearably. *Dragon . . . What did she know of dragons? And the dragon's lyre . . . ?* He had never heard of a dragon's lyre, yet something stirred his memory to racing, and bard knowledge exploded, wanting to free itself.

"What is the dragon's lyre?"

"The dragon's lyre—the ivory lyre of the dragon called Bayzun," she said dreamily.

The word "Bayzun" struck like fire through Teb, tumbling his thoughts.

He tried to collect his wits. He had no knowledge of such a lyre or of a dragon named Bayzun, yet his blood pounded at the words. Then the knowledge did surface, powers beat at him until soon the whole tale of the lyre had released itself from the dark side of memory.

The Ivory Lyre of Bayzun. Yes, he could picture it now—a small white lyre no bigger than the length of his two hands, a delicate lyre, its strings spun of silver and its thin fretwork carved with great skill. Carved from the ivory claws of a huge dragon, the ivory fitted together cleverly. The lyre was carved from the claws of Bayzun, the grandfather of all singing dragons.

He knew the lyre was lost. He knew that all knowledge of it had been wiped away from the minds of men, from the minds of all bards and dragons. He knew the spell that hid it had broken at this instant, because of his questioning. *If one bard or dragon among us seeks it, the memory will come alive.*

"Is the lyre here in Dacia?" he asked carefully.

She nodded.

The lyre had power, great power. It had once been known to all Tirror. Knowledge of the dwarf who had carved it, and of the dragon who had given his claws for its making, filled Teb's mind.

But another knowledge touched him, too, woven into the tale of the lyre. There was one object, a stone tablet, that breached the spell on the lyre. It told the tale of the lyre and its powers. That tablet, too, must be here in Dacia. It was the only way the king—and Accacia—could know about the lyre.

He must find the lyre. The tablet was of no importance now that the spell was broken. But the lyre . . .

The Ivory Lyre of Bayzun could give him and the dragons forces they had not yet touched, to defeat the dark rulers.

Accacia stirred. "I see you have heard of the lyre."

"I have never heard of it," he said truthfully. "But its very name sounds magical, and by your look and the way you speak of it, it must have power."

"It is a small lyre carved from the claws of the grandfather of all singing dragons—if you believe in such creatures."

"I have heard they are extinct. If they ever existed."

"I hope they are extinct. They could be very harmful to us. The power of the lyre itself is sufficient for us to keep the dark at bay." She was becoming more aware once again as his own concentration lagged. He thought of Garit—if he could find Garit this night, what news he would have for him. He brought his force so strong his palms began to sweat.

"Where is the lyre, Accacia?"

"Sardira . . . moves it from place to place," she said dreamily. "Treasure rooms . . . all over the palace."

But he knew where it was now, or had been recently. It was that bright magic that had called to him from behind the locked oak door that guarded the upper treasure room. "How did King Sardira come by such a power?" he asked softly.

"It . . . I don't know how it came here. A warrior brought it, I think. Such things, such dead facts, are of no importance." She sighed. "The lyre has the power to drive back the dark enough so it cannot conquer Dacia. Power—if King Sardira were to take up arms against Quazelzeg and the dark lords, enough power, perhaps, even to conquer them."

Teb stared.

"Sardira," Accacia said softly, "prefers that the lyre stand as talisman only, a wall against the dark's ultimate power. In this way, Dacia can take advantage of the dark's power in safety. Dacia can take advantage of both sides, and yet remain free of both."

Teb studied her, understanding Sardira's purpose too well. A delicate balance between the perversions Dacia enjoyed in the company of the dark and Dacia's total enslavement. The dark would not know what caused that power, would only know that some force stood against them.

"If the lyre did not exist, Accacia, and Dacia were enslaved, what would you do then?"

Her eyes were lidded with sleepiness. "I would still have my life as I choose. I would still have the luxuries I want."

"You would be a . . . friend to the dark?"

"Yes."

"And the dark would not crush you?"

She smiled. "I please the dark leaders."

"And the lyre is kept safe," he said softly, pulling her to him, "within the king's treasuries. How many treasuries are there?"

"Several. Seven . . . eight." Her voice was growing

very sleepy. "Some very deep . . . deep in the core of the mountain, guarded . . . guarded by the fanged lizards."

"How would one reach such chambers?"

"Deep passages, a complicated way . . ." She kissed him lazily and subsided into a dreaminess that he did not, again, try to lift.

He sat a moment thinking of the lyre, then of Garit and the plans they could now make. Then he rose, pulled Accacia up and led her as one would lead a child, out of the garden and through halls lit only by her lantern. He left her in an empty reception room near where he could see the king and the un-men taking mithnon. He hoped he had blocked all memory of her words from her. She would find her way to more exciting company now.

He thought about Nightraider riding the winds alone, searching for Camery. As he went along to his chambers to change into his old leathers, excitement filled him that he might see Camery this night, that maybe Nightraider had already found her. Or maybe she had escaped Ekthuma and found her way to Garit. He would go down into the city, to Garit first, then to the stadium where the cats were held. Before he reached the stables, he found the three dragons waiting for him in the forms of wolves.

They made their way quickly over the route the mounted entourage had taken, skirting clutches of revelers and drunks and cadheads. No one bothered them, most backed away from the wolves, for these were not

150

blinded creatures pulling carts, but fierce and snarling. Teb kept to the darkest shadows so his face would not be remembered.

He found Garit's cottage, making sure by the position of the tower. The windows were dark, no crack of light. The steps were rickety, the front porch littered with rubble. He knocked softly. When no one answered, he went around to the back door and rapped again. There was no crack of light here, either, no sign that anyone was inside. After a few minutes he tried the door, found it locked, returned to the front. That door, too, was bolted.

He tried a shutter and found it securely fastened. He didn't want to break in. He thought of leaving Garit some message, a few words scrawled on a board with a stick, but he didn't want it found by someone else. He left at last, flattened with disappointment, the wolves walking close now in sympathy.

At the stadium they could hear a huge commotion. A crowd of men was shouting and slamming gates. Starpounder slipped in through a dark side gate to look, his wolf form hidden in shadow. He returned to say a band of soldiers was unloading several bulls and some guard lizards from carts drawn up inside the arena. *There are too many, Tebriel. We will attract too much attention. We must return later, when they have gone.*

Yes, Seastrider said. *In the small hours when no one is here, we will release the cats, then go to Garit. Now let us be off to the sky. Wolf forms are not comfortable, and this city stinks.*

They found a hill above the ruins where they would not be seen. The three began to change, the wolf forms to grow thin, then transparent.

But they did not turn to dragons. They remained wolves, thin as cloud, so the rough grass showed through. It was a long time before Seastrider's true dragon shape began to waver over the thin wolf form, huge but only mist—as if the change into wolf had taken the last of a strangely waning strength. Teb tried to help her. The other two looked on, shadows of wolves.

Slowly Seastrider grew denser. Her wings showed thinly against the sky. She became almost solid, she tried to lift, she flew clumsily—then she faltered and fell to earth like a crippled bird, becoming only wolf again.

The other two had not changed. Teb felt their effort, but the evil on them was too powerful. They were trapped, shivering, their wolf eyes flashing. But they all kept trying, Teb with every ounce of power in him. At long last, when he thought it was useless, Seastrider began to find her shape again, stronger now until she coiled across the hill like thickening mist, turning whiter, denser, slowly gaining solid form.

At last she was a solid, living dragon.

She breathed out flame slowly, testing herself. Teb hugged her, pressing his face against her cheek. Soon Starpounder began to change, then Windcaller.

The dragons lifted skyward into the night, shaken, reaching with trembling effort for the clouds.

"Was it on purpose?" Teb shouted into the wind later. "Did the unliving do that on purpose? Do they know about you?"

"No, Tebriel. I think not. But there is more evil upon Dacia, now the unliving are here."

Once the dragons were away from Dacia and out over the sea, their strength returned. They hunted shark and fed, coiled on a marshy island. Here they spoke together of the lyre of Bayzun, for the knowledge had flooded into the minds of the dragons when it burst into Teb's own conscious thought.

"The spell is broken," Seastrider said. "The spell Bayzun himself laid upon the lyre has been fulfilled." She eased into a new position among the boulders. Teb shifted, too, to find the warmest spot against her scaly side.

"The lyre was fashioned from the claws of Bayzun," Seastrider said. "Three claws he tore from his own foot as he lay old and weak, knowing he would soon die.

"Bayzun called forth the dwarf Eppennen, master carver of all the dwarfs of the northern lands, and bade him carve the lyre as he instructed. Eppennen did the work there in Bayzun's own cave, never leaving until the lyre was completed, taking for his meals the small creatures that Bayzun was still able to kill. When Eppennen completed the lyre, Bayzun clasped it to his scaly chest and said spells over it to enhance its magic.

"The lyre was used only once," Seastrider said, "against the first dark invaders. Its powers are against

153

dark magic, Tebriel, not against normal human force. It will not weaken a warrior, but it will weaken the dark evils that drive him. It will strengthen the force of the bard magic. It will strengthen dragon song and the visions we make.

"When the first unliving tried to take the minds of Tirror and destroy the bards and dragons, Bayzun rose up with the last of his great strength and sang, clutching the lyre to his chest with his clawless foot. He drove the dark out with the lyre's magic—his own power and the lyre together drove it out, a power that shattered the dark across Tirror. . . .

"The dark retreated back into other worlds for a while, though it would come again. Bayzun laid the lyre upon a pile of leaves that often pillowed his head. There it remained until Bayzun was mortally wounded by the spear of an evil man come secretly in the night, killing Bayzun when he was too weak to defend himself, stealing the lyre.

"But before he died," Seastrider said, "Bayzun laid a curse on the lyre: that even if the dark held it, the dark could never use its power. All the dark could do in holding the lyre would be to prevent its use by the dragons and bards . . . or by anyone who would defeat the dark with it.

"Then," she said, her breath spurting little flames, "then the un-men laid a countercurse: that the history of the lyre of Bayzun, and of Bayzun himself, would vanish from all bard memory and from the memory of all dragons, from the memory of all men and animals.

He did not know that the dwarf had carved a tablet telling of the lyre.

"In his last gasping breath, Bayzun's curse was the final one: that there would come a time when the dragons and bards would come together in force once more. At the beginning of that time the memory of the lyre would come alive again, if even one among us sought it.

"You sought it, Tebriel. Now," she said, turning her long silver head to look at him, "now we must recover it from the treasure halls of Sardira. All dragons will know of the lyre, now the spell is spent. Dawncloud will know. All bards will know. . . . Your mother, your sister . . ."

"But how did the tablet get out of the cave to the palace where the lyre is? How did the lyre itself . . . ?"

"You know all that I know, Tebriel. There are still mysteries shrouded by the presence of the dark. But I see the dwarf Eppennen returning to that cave, to the corpse of Bayzun, and carrying the tablet away." Seastrider licked a morsel of shark from her claws. "You will find the lyre, Tebriel. You will . . . among the treasure rooms of Sardira. Your powers are growing stronger. You concealed your true self at supper tonight very well. And you laid a strong mind-spell on Accacia."

He touched her pearl-colored nose. "How much *do* you see, lurking in your disguise in the stable?"

"Quite enough." He could feel her silent laugh like a small earthquake. "Sometimes I sense your thoughts clearly in spite of the aura of the dark; sometimes I do not. Though I sensed quite enough tonight to tell me that Lady Accacia's flirting and her charm undoes you."

"If it undoes me," he said crossly, "how would I have been able to lay sufficient spell on her to learn of the ivory lyre?"

"I have trained you well," she said smugly.

He leaped at her and pummeled her until she took his shoulder in her sharp fangs. He held still then, staring up at her eyes, like two green lakes above him. She did not press down even enough to dent his skin. When she released him, he jumped to her back and they were airborne in a wild release of craziness. She dove and spun, then beat out fast across the night winds, freeing them both in flight as wild as hurricanes.

She dove so close to waves that Teb was drenched, and soared so high he grew faint from the thin air. Windcaller and Starpounder did not follow them, and there was no sense of Nightraider on the night sky. The black dragon followed his search in deliberate isolation, all his strength turned toward one being.

At last Seastrider returned to Dacia. They both felt strengthened now by their absence from the dark power concentrated there. They felt ready to face it again. Teb's mind was filled with the captive animals, and with Garit and Camery.

He had no idea whether the underground knew the

great cats had been captured. He had no plan. But as Seastrider circled the stadium, they heard the harsh, angry scream of a great cat, wild with pain. Teb stiffened, touched his sword, staring down at the dark arena.

CHAPTER

14

Seastrider dove so the stadium leaped up at Teb out of blackness. The cat screamed again. Teb smelled burning fur. They hovered over the stands. Metal rattled; a man laughed. They could see two figures at a small fire at one end of the arena. The bars of cages shone in the firelight. Chained animals crouched behind them, eyes flashing as a third figure thrust a red hot poker through. A great cat leaped away from it screaming, choked by the chain that held it against the bars.

I can dive on them, Seastrider said.

No. The whole city would soon know there are dragons. The main gate is ajar; I can get in there.

Seastrider chose a deserted hill beyond the stadium, littered with fallen, rotted buildings and broken walls, just above the river. She dropped down. "I will go with you."

He slid down from her back. "The white mare would be recognized. A wolf is too small, and maybe you

158

couldn't change back. Go up, Seastrider, into the clouds."

"I will try another shape. A bear—yes, I remember bears; there are songs that hold the bears' essence." She breathed out a snort of flame, and before he could argue, the night rippled and twisted, the dragon shimmered, faded, and a dark hulk reared over Teb, a blackness against the stars reaching out at him with broad paws, growling.

When she dropped to all fours, he grabbed a handful of her shaggy coat and swung aboard. She sped down the hill at a fast rolling gait. He could see by the first touch of dawn that her coat was not dark, but silver. He had never smelled a bear—it was pungent and wild. The cat screamed again. Seastrider reached the high wall. The iron gate was just ajar. She shouldered through. Teb drew his sword as they swung toward the fire. Before they were within its light, he slipped down.

Beyond the fire the cat twisted, screaming, away from the burning poker. Teb leaped for the fire, grabbed one of the men, and stabbed him. The bear tumbled the other, mauling him and muffling his screams. The man at the cages turned to look, but before Teb could reach him, a figure appeared out of nowhere, out of the dark, leaping to the torturer's back. There was a cry, Teb saw the flash of a knife. By the time he reached the fight, the torturer lay writhing and the smaller figure was running for the gate.

Teb knelt over the soldier, glancing back toward the fire, where the bear was flinging one of the dead soldiers into the air, catching and battering him. He stared into the dying soldier's face for a moment, a youth no older than he but sallow and evil, even in death. He removed the knife, wiped it clean, and put it in his belt, where it would not identify its owner; then he watched the soldier die.

He opened the gates to the cages and unchained the five big cats and two wolves. No creature spoke; they moved out quickly toward the gate, crowding around the bear as if for safety. Beyond the gate they found the river quickly, and the animals crouched among rubble and broken walls to drink. Panting, the five big cats shivered with pain. The two wolves slunk as no speaking animal should. The silver bear stood rearing beside them, watching the stadium they had left and the barracks that formed one side of it, turning her head back and forth, listening. When no sound came from the stadium, she sat down at last and contemplated the animals. One of the great cats came to her and Teb, limping badly. Her voice was hardly a breath.

She was the sand-colored cat he had released first, her body torn with fresh burns. She raised her face to Teb, her green eyes caressing him, then licked his face, leaning her head against him. At last she stood back, studying Teb and the bear appraisingly.

"If you were riding a marvelous white mare, I would think you Prince Tebmund of Thorley. But instead, you ride a bear. . . . Do bears speak, my prince? I have never known a bear."

He laughed. "This bear speaks. She is . . . kin to the white mare, you might say."

The cat twitched a whisker. "I am Elmmira of the colony of Gardel-Cloor. We are in your debt. Do you know whether the girl escaped safely?"

"What girl?"

"The girl with the knife, who killed the soldier."

"She got out the gate safely. Who was she?"

"That must remain our secret, even though you saved us. We would not speak her name without her permission." Elmmira laid a soft paw against his chest. "My companions are Domma, Jimmica, Xemmos, and Jerymm." Each animal lifted its head as Elmmira spoke its name. "Our wolf friends were brought here as captives from Igness. Yallel and Zellig."

"I am Tebmund of Thorley." Teb felt ashamed at giving these animals less than the truth. But if the great cats felt the need for care, then so should he. "The bear does not give her name. But tell me of Gardel-Cloor. That is an ancient sanctuary. Are you free to tell me where it lies?"

"That, too, Prince Tebmund, we cannot reveal even to you." Elmmira began to lick at her burns. The bear turned to look at the animals, then started up over the rubble-strewn hill. They followed, Teb walking among them. But soon the sky began to grow lighter, the bear's silver shape becoming too visible among the fallen houses.

"You'll be seen if you stay with us," Teb told the

animals. "Go quickly where you can hide, before Sardira sends out his soldiers. He'll be in a rage that you escaped; he'll get you back if he can."

The animals raised their faces to him for a moment, exchanged a long look with the bear, then angled off quickly among the broken walls and ran, limping, down toward the city and the sea cliffs. Teb did not see Elmmira pause, sniff for scent among the rubble, then begin to track. He swung onto the bear's back and she moved at a fast, rolling walk up over the hill. An empty valley lay beyond, rocky and desolate. Here the bear plunged down, in a hurry now to change back and take to the sky before dawn grew too light.

But in the valley she paused, agitated. Teb slipped down. She began to pace, lumbering around boulders, fighting something unseen. She returned to Teb at last, her head down, shifting and backing uncomfortably. *I cannot change. I am trapped, Tebriel.*

He tried to help. It did no good. Seastrider remained solidly a bear. Teb mounted at last and they went on, up the cliff and onto open fields, back toward the course of the river. It was too light now for her to take to the sky, even could she have changed. In the shadows of a dense grove they hid themselves—if such a huge, pale creature could hide anywhere. She squeezed into the brambles, Teb lying along her back, his head against her rough coat, trying with her, trying to change. . . .

She clawed at the earth, combing ridges into the soft forest mulch. She pressed her shoulder against a huge oak, forcing to bring the magic, then in an agony of defeat she raked great gashes down its bark so the wood beneath shone white in four long strokes. And still she was a bear. The morning had come. Down below the wood they could hear the city waking, bangs and thumps and voices calling, and a squeaky cart.

The silver bear ceased fighting the dark. Teb slid from her back. She faced him, very still. *I will go away alone. Far from here across the inlets south, away from the forces of the unliving. I will swim the sea to some deserted shore, then I will be able to change back.*

You won't go alone.

Yes.

I won't let you go alone; we must not be separated. Come . . .

Instead of arguing or letting him mount, she spun fast for her bulk, her teeth bared and her ears laid flat, her roar heavy with fury. He stepped back with amazement, his arm up to shield his face, then he saw the horsemen advancing on them from out of the dark forest: It was them the silver bear faced. As they circled bear and prince, they threw their leather capes back to show the yellow uniforms beneath. In the lead rode Captain Leskrank, General Vurbane, and black-robed King Sardira.

Calm, Teb thought. *Calm. Put a good face on it.*

Yes, calm, Tebriel. A pet bear, a guard bear raised in Thedria . . .

"You're out early," Teb said. "You've discovered my secret at last. I had thought not to burden you with my pet." He grinned. "She is not the sort of animal I would have brought into the palace with me."

They sat looking down at him, Sardira's face a pale thin moon above black robe and black horse, General Vurbane like a melted wax figure where the scar made his face run together. Heavy-shouldered, hunched Leskrank glowered at Teb and the bear, his waxen face pale and eager with the promise of torture. Twelve soldiers flanked them, their horses backing and fighting to stay away from the bear.

"It is not the sort of animal," King Sardira said, "that exists in this hemisphere, Prince Tebmund. Tell us how you came by it."

"Oh, they exist." Teb smiled. "We raise them on Thedria and train them as guard animals. I understand that in the nations of Windthorst they use winged jackals, but we find the bears more . . . accommodating. Do not fear her; she is quite tame unless danger threatens. She has been most obedient about staying here to herself, in the wood."

"There are no bears on Thedria," said Vurbane. "I have been there. There is no Prince Tebmund, either."

"Oh, there are bears," Teb said lightly. "There is no Prince Tebmund, of course, for I am here."

Vurbane looked annoyed, a drawing-back deep within his cold eyes; Teb hoped he had been bluffing.

"When were you in Thedria?" Teb asked lightly. "I do not remember your visit, General Vurbane."

Vurbane did not answer, but only stared at Teb, then nodded briefly to King Sardira. Sardira motioned to Leskrank, a quick, irritated movement. Leskrank raised a hand, and at once the soldiers spurred their reluctant horses forward, their swords a circle of steel pointing down at Teb and Seastrider; the bear reared and charged the horses, clawing one and snatching the rider from the saddle. Teb's sword cut down two soldiers as their horses spun, trying to bolt. He turned to see spears bristling at the bear as she lunged at Captain Leskrank, spears ready to sink deep. "No!" he cried. "No!" *There are too many. Fall back.*

She hesitated, and a spear pierced her shoulder. *Fall back!* At last she dropped to all fours, the points of a dozen spears pricking her heavy coat.

A rider dismounted and took Teb's sword and tied his hands behind him. He tied a long rope around Teb's neck, gave Sardira the other end, and kicked Teb in the ankle. "Get moving." Teb walked out fast beside the bear. Sardira spurred his horse so close it nearly trampled Teb, then jogged ahead so Teb had to run or be dragged. Double-time they went down along the river past derelict farms, then through the rubbled streets. As they approached the arena, Sardira jerked Teb to a stop and sat glaring down at him.

"Tell me why you released my animals, Prince Tebmund. Why would you do such a thing after we treated you so hospitably?"

Teb stared at the king and said nothing.

"Who was your accomplice, Prince Tebmund? Oh, yes, my men saw him; they saw it all from the barracks. They saw him run away. They came down here to find three of my best soldiers murdered."

Teb looked at the king coldly. "I suppose it is some special privilege for your *best* soldiers, to be allowed to torture helpless animals."

The king cut him a look of cold disgust. "I suppose *you* are some sort of judge. Do you bleed for every slaughtered sheep on the supper table, Prince Tebmund?"

Teb only looked at him.

"You don't imagine, *Prince* Tebmund, that I believed your story about coming here only to sell horses. *Whom* do you spy for, *Prince* Tebmund? Some gutter-based cadre of self-made rebels itching to be slaughtered by my armies?"

Teb stared in silence, up into Sardira's cold, black eyes.

"Well, your tale about trading horses will be honored, *Prince* Tebmund—if you are a prince—but your payment will not be quite what you planned. It will be payment to match the intent. . . ."

Teb looked the king over coldly, then spat on the sword and shouldered it out of his way as another blade probed his back. He sauntered through the gate beside the ambling silver bear, his fury so hot his blood throbbed like drums.

. . . *to advantage,* Seastrider was saying. *Go easy, Tebriel. We will use this to advantage, I will get my power back. . . . Three dragons are still free, to help us. . . .*

But Teb could not sense the others; there was no

166

answering surge that showed they were linked by thought. Nothing.

They were marched the length of the gaming field and forced into cages. Teb was chained, but no soldier would enter the bear's cage. Her door was bolted and locked. Four mounted soldiers were left to guard them and to prepare them for the games.

CHAPTER

15

Kiri huddled against a broken wall in an old stone ruin, sick with pain where the soldier had stabbed her, dizzy with the loss of blood. She listened for the sound of running feet, pressing at the wound in her side to stop the bleeding. At last she knelt, tore a strip off her skirt, and bound the long gash so tightly she could hardly breathe. She had foolishly left her knife in the soldier. She hoped he was dead, but she wished she had it back.

She thought the creature in the arena must have been a bear; but there were no more bears on this side of the world. And who was the man with it? Where had he come from, there in the lonely arena in the small hours of night?

She turned to look up the rubble-strewn hill and caught her breath. There he was, a black silhouette in the first touch of dawn, riding the huge bear and followed by a tangle of fast-moving shapes that she soon made out to be Elmmira, the other cats, and maybe wolves. It was too dark to see his face. She wanted to follow, to call out, and knew she mustn't be seen. If she was caught out in the open, wounded, they would soon know who stabbed the king's soldier. She felt so weak. Even her vision seemed blurred. She needed shelter, needed someone to help her. She knew the cats would go to Gardel-Cloor and longed to go with them, but she mustn't be seen with them. They would have care at Gardel-Cloor, rest, and salves for the burns. Marshy was there, with Summer.

She moved out of the ruined building at last and on through the rubble, supporting herself against broken walls. When she felt faint again, she leaned on a partial stair rail, then sat down on the bottom of three standing steps, her head between her knees until the sickness went away.

At last the ruins ended. She forced herself out onto the open streets where a few people were at the cow pens or emptying dirty water into the gutters. She dared not go home so close to the palace; a neighbor could report that she was wounded. She did not want to draw attention to Gram. She didn't think she could make it down the steep cliff to Gardel-Cloor.

Only Garit could help her, yet she was terrified of being followed there, covered with blood. It was true dawn now, far too light. She caught a woman staring at her, and at the next corner she snatched a heavy shirt from a fence rail and slipped it over her tunic. It was still damp from laundering, and chilly. She felt dizzy again, confused. What street was this? Why didn't it look familiar? She leaned against a stone wall, trying to get her bearings. She thought she was going to throw up; everything around her seemed smeared and unclear. When a shadow moved nearby, she froze. Was someone following her? She crouched against a wall, the pain making her gasp, and searched for shelter ahead. Behind her the shadow moved again. She caught her breath. . . .

It was Elmmira. The great cat leaped to join her, pressing against her. "Come on my back; be quick."

She slipped onto Elmmira's back as easily as she could, trying not to touch the horrible burns, and hot tears filled her eyes at Elmmira's pain, that the great cat would do this when she herself should be cared for. She clung to the rhythm of Elmmira's gallop, her nostrils filled with the smell of burnt fur, two crippled creatures fleeing through the city. A shout behind them made Elmmira swerve, running flat out. Kiri lay low as they dodged down a narrow alley and around corners. The jarring sent jabs of pain through Kiri; then Elmmira leaped so high Kiri barely stayed with her. They had gone over a fence. When Elmmira stopped suddenly, Kiri thought they were cornered; then she heard Garit's voice.

She felt herself lifted, the pain searing her.

She remembered nothing more until she woke with bright sun seeping through the shutters. She was in Garit's bed, the covers pulled up warm. Garit sat watching her.

"Where is Elmmira?" Kiri cried. "Did she get away?"

"She is safe—all the cats are. They are gone from the city down into Gardel-Cloor, and the poor wolves, too."

"But they—"

"No one will find them in the tunnels. There is power there, Kiri, in the stone."

"But they need doctoring. The burns . . ."

"Marshy and Summer are there with them. I have been down, and taken roots for the salve."

She started to raise up but pain flared in her side. She felt the pull of bandages as she settled back into the pillows. "Did Elmmira tell you what happened?"

"Yes."

"A man was there in the stadium with a huge animal—a bear. They killed two soldiers. I might be dead now, but for them. Who was he, Garit? They didn't catch him? Did he get away?"

He put his hand over hers. "Too many questions. You must rest. The young man escaped on the back of a great silver bear."

She sighed. "I might have helped him, I might have stayed. I knew he would release the cats—why else would he come? When I felt the knife in me and the blood flowing, all I could think was, I mustn't be found there dead. . . . Because of Papa, that it would link him to the resistance."

"Yes, I know, Kiri."

"But he released the animals? They all got away? Who was he?"

"He released them all. It was Prince Tebmund."

171

She stared at Garit. "Then he *is* your Prince of Auric. He *is* Tebriel."

"There is no real proof of that. Here, drink this broth. I am roasting a calf's liver for you, for strength."

She accepted the bowl of broth and breathed in its steamy fragrance. She began to sip it, then sucked it in greedily.

When she had finished, she lay watching Garit as he turned the roasting liver over a small bed of coals.

"It may have been Tebriel," he said. "It may not." But his eyes were bright with hope.

Her head began to feel clearer, and she remembered she had something to tell Garit. "I was coming to tell you . . . something important . . . but I passed near Elmmira's den and saw her in the trap, and . . ."

"What were you coming to tell me?" he said gently.

She sat up despite the pain and held out her hand to him. He came to sit on the edge of the bed.

"I listened to Prince Tebmund and Accacia talking last night. He made her say things, Garit. It was amazing—I thought he laid a spell on her." She gripped his hand hard, filled with excitement. "Do you know why the dark cannot enslave Dacia?"

"I thought it simply would not. That it found Dacia a more convenient go-between as it is."

"There is another reason."

He waited.

"The dark *cannot*, Garit. There is a talisman of power there in the palace, more powerful than Gardel-Cloor. It is the Ivory Lyre of Bayzun."

He shook his head. The words meant nothing to him. She described the lyre for him, described the ancient dragon laying his spells. She felt a chill of wonder at the way the story had come suddenly, whole, into her mind as she stood peering into the dark garden. It must have come into Colewolf's mind at the same moment, and Summer's and Marshy's, too. The spell of forgetting had been broken when one bard sought the truth. She knew she must be that bard, come to listen, hiding behind the pierced black screen.

"But," Garit said, "whether the king was given the lyre or found it quite by accident, he would not have known what it was, not known about its power . . . unless there was some written record."

"There was a carved tablet, made by the dwarf who watched Bayzun die. But how Sardira got that tablet, I don't know."

They stared at each other, both filled with the meaning such power would have, to destroy the dark forces. "We must have it," Garit said. "We must have the lyre."

"Yes." She lay back, dizzy and weak again, her mind gone foggy. Then slowly a sense of terrible distress filled her, so she reached out blindly, clutching at air.

"What is it? *Kiri?*" His face seemed to swim before her, concerned, frightened. "What is happening? *Kiri?*"

"I . . . don't know. Something . . ." She had a sense of huge crowds, deafening noise, could feel chains binding her and felt she was clutching at iron bars, felt rage not her own. . . .

173

Then, as suddenly, it was gone. She stared at Garit, confused.

"The stadium," she whispered, her throat tight. "I don't know what—or who. Garit, something is happening at the stadium. Someone needs help." She felt as if forces like ripples in water were reaching out to snare her thoughts. "It is the lyre," she said, "the power of the broken spell, helping me see." She turned on her side clutching the pillow, hurting and dizzy, watched vaguely as Garit pulled on his boots and strapped on his sword. Their eyes met.

"I was about to go there," he said, "when you woke. Our people are there, all our forces. What did you see in vision, Kiri? Can you tell me?"

"Chains. And bars . . . someone is chained in the cages."

His eyes showed fear. His face tightened. He moved to the window and pulled a shutter open enough to see the sky. "There is time," he said. "They will do nothing to . . . a prisoner until the games begin. Another hour or more."

She pushed her covers back. "Too warm. I will eat the broiled liver now; then I'll feel better—as strong as the stadium bulls."

"Not strong enough to go out. I expect you to stay here while I'm gone."

"No. I'm going with you."

"You're not fit."

"I am, and I'm hungry."

He sliced the liver and brought it to her with two

slabs of buttered bread. It tasted so good she had to stop herself from wolfing it. There was milk, too, and an apple. Garit was sharpening his knife. Her mind was still filled with the vision, powerful and frightening. It was no good to wonder who was caged; they would find out soon enough. Her thoughts turned to the lyre's spell . . . then she caught her breath.

Memory of the lyre will live again when dragons and bards come together. . . .

But there were no more dragons. No dragons . . . If there had been dragons, they would have come to find their bards. The rest of the spell had happened, though. . . .

When even one among them seeks it . . . Yes, she had sought that knowledge and broken the spell as she stood behind the screen eavesdropping on Accacia and Prince Tebmund . . . Tebriel. . . .

Or had she?

She had only been eavesdropping. She had not actively sought that knowledge.

But Tebriel *had* sought it. He had made Accacia talk, had questioned her pointedly. He had sought very specific knowledge. It was Tebriel's power that had made Accacia tell about the lyre. Tebriel . . . had sought it. . . . She raised up to stare at Garit.

"Who *is* he, Garit? *Who is Tebriel?*"

He turned to look at her.

"You didn't tell me all of it."

"There is a mark on his arm," he said. "I thought not to tell you until I was sure it was Teb. There is

175

the mark—of the dragon. On his left arm, just here," he said, pointing to a place halfway between wrist and elbow on the inside of his left arm.

She frowned, then shook her head. "There is a scar there. I saw it when I looked at his horses. I didn't notice a mark."

"It is very small—perhaps a scar would hide it. You looked at his horses?"

"Yes."

"And how did they respond to you?"

"They were loving. Sweet and nuzzling and dear. But I've heard they're not that way with the soldiers. And they hate Accacia. I watched through a crack in the barn and thought the big black stallion would kill her."

Garit looked at her strangely but said nothing.

She stared back at him, her mind filled with Tebriel . . . *dragonbard.* . . . "I must find him, Garit. No," she said, seeing his face, "*I* want to do it. I must. I will ask the proper questions. I will make sure. . . . The bright tapestries of other worlds, his mother's favorite color, his pony, Linnet . . . *I want to find him.* . . ." *Dragonbard* . . .

"There is another who would know him, Kiri. Without asking questions."

"You would, of course. But Garit, he—"

"Another besides myself." He sat down on the bed and took her hand. "If he is Tebriel, Summer will know him."

176

She studied his face. "You mean because Summer is a bard? But so am I. He . . ." Her mind was filled again with that powerful vision of the stadium, of chains and bars, and now with much more, for now she knew who was chained there and her pulse pounded with urgency. She sat only half listening to Garit, knowing the prisoner was the prince . . . Tebriel . . . dragonbard . . . caged and chained in the stadium.

"Summer is Tebriel's sister, Kiri. His sister—"

She could hardly attend to Garit. "But . . . Summer comes from Zinsan."

"No. That is only the story we used to protect her. Summer is Tebriel's sister. Her name is Camery. I brought her away from imprisonment in the tower of Auric when she was fourteen. But you— Kiri, are you all right?"

"He *is* Tebriel. He is a dragonbard. It was he who broke the spell of the lyre, not me. It is he in the stadium, he who made the vision of bars and chains . . . asking for help—"

They were interrupted by a soft brushing against the door. Garit peered out through a crack, then pulled the door open. The great cat pushed in, the big-boned tom with the black-brown coat, and eyes like yellow moons.

"Xemmos!" Garit said. "What— You all should be hidden in Gardel-Cloor. The stadium games . . ."

"That is why I have come. Word came by way of an escaping wolf. Prince Tebmund of Thedria has been taken prisoner, along with his great bear. He is chained in a cage at the stadium and the bear locked into a cage next to him."

There was no more talk; Garit left at once for the stadium, pulling on a loose leather coat to hide his short crossbow and sword. Xemmos leaped away to return to Gardel-Cloor, to fetch Summer. Kiri rose and dressed in a leather tunic that would cover the bandages and cover a short sword. Perhaps it would also hide the fact that she walked bent over, from the pain. War would begin today, she felt certain of it. Their forces, no matter how unready, could not allow the murder of a dragonbard in the stadium games.

She went as quickly as she could, gritting her teeth against the pain, through streets now nearly deserted. As she neared the stadium, the noise was deafening, for nearly the entire city crowded to get in. She hated the ugliness of this and felt her stomach quease with sickness.

She had served as page in the king's plush private box—at Accacia's request—often enough to have had her fill of the screaming and blood. Nothing ever died quickly; all was drawn out so the dark leaders, always present, could take ultimate pleasure in the pain and terror. She had stood beside the purple satin drapings that lined the king's box, seeing Accacia's laughing face, wondering how her cousin could bear it.

She had always wanted to find gentleness in Accacia, and kindness, but she never had. She shouldered through the outer crowds, showed herself to a guard who was one of their own, and slipped through the little gate ahead of everyone else. Catcalls and jeers followed her for her special privilege, but likely they only thought she was a prostitute currying the guard's favor. Her cheeks burned at that thought. Ahead, beyond the milling, shouting crowd, she could see the tops of the barred cages.

16

The fox abandoned subtlety and manners, and gave the sleeping queen a sharp poke. "Wake up! It's Hexet!"

The queen stirred, brushing at her thin, tangled white hair, looked up over the mass of blankets, and scowled at him. "Go away. Don't poke me. Where are your manners? Come back when you can speak softly, the way I like."

Gently, he laid a paw on her cheek and looked deep into her pale eyes. He would like to nip her and rout her out of that bed. "Wake up properly. It's urgent—something vital and urgent."

She sat up in a storm of blankets and stared at him. "I don't like *urgent.* Or *vital.*" But she put out her thin old hand to him and stroked his back. "What is it? What is this all about? I've never seen you so—"

"Agitated," he supplied. "I am agitated and angry, and you must get up out of that bed at once."

"Are you telling me what I must do? I am a queen. You are only—"

"A dignitary in my own nation," he said, "and equally as important as you. And far more useful to the world, considering our respective talents."

"What does that mean? You are making double-talk."

"I am only speaking the truth." He settled down into the pile of covers, nuzzled her cheek gently, then placed a soft paw against her thin lips. "Now listen. I will tell you something, and I don't want interruptions. It must be told, Queen Stephana. And you must listen." He removed his paw and sat looking at her.

She started to tell him there was nothing she *must* do, then changed her mind and settled back against the headboard, sighing, pulling the blankets around her.

He bobbed his chin with satisfaction. "It is about Prince Tebmund. You told me he had visited with you."

Her face went closed with apprehension. She searched his face, then nodded reluctantly.

"Did you like him? Did you feel kinship with him?"

Her eyes blazed, as if he had spoken of something private that was not his right to consider.

"Did you?"

"What if I did. He is a nice enough young man."

"What kinship, Queen Stephana? There is not much time. Do you know what kind of kinship?" He watched her, saw the spark of fear in her eyes. She did not want to discuss this. Yet he saw something more, too. Something strange, alien to her. He saw tears start.

"He is the same as you, Queen Stephana. He is a dragonbard."

Despite the tears, her eyes went wild at this effrontery. And with this truth, for she could not deny it. He moved closer, touching her with his nose.

"Prince Tebmund has been taken captive. He is chained in the stadium."

Her eyes flew open.

"The king intends to use him in the games. He will die today, Queen Stephana, if you do not get up out of that bed and help him."

"Die?" She breathed, her eyes searching and wild. Then her look was shuttered. She lifted her chin and regarded him steadily. "I can do nothing. What could I do?"

He stared at her in silence.

"What difference if he dies?" she shouted suddenly, her anger seeming to make her grow larger. "What difference? What good is he? What good am I?" She stared at Hexet, furious. Then, in a whisper, "What good is a dragonbard without . . . without dragons?" Her anger boiled out again. "That part of the prophecy was wrong! There are no more dragons!" She fixed Hexet with a defiant stare. Then she shrank into herself, and sat cowering in her blankets.

"What prophecy?" he said sharply. "What are you talking about?" Then, at her silence, "You must tell me. Is it a prophecy that has to do with Prince Tebmund? With dragonbards—with yourself? Where did you hear it?" He watched her, tense with excitement. "You must tell me. You must!

"Only you can help him," Hexet said softly. "If you do not, they will kill him."

He saw she was weakening. "His murder will be a curse on your soul, Queen Stephana."

She stared at him in misery. He pushed his nose against her cold hands, but his look was hard, demanding.

At last she seemed to relax, to soften, to give up the battle. Her eyes were pained, and somehow younger. And then, so suddenly that she startled him, she was weeping, deep, racking sobs that alarmed him.

He had never seen her so out of control. Had she taken some of the drug? Roderica kept it here, did not put it into her food, took it herself sometimes, which explained, Hexet thought, Roderica's wild changes in temperament. He pressed against the queen, and the old woman put her arms around him and bawled wetly into his shoulder.

When she subsided at last, she told him about the lyre, how the sudden knowledge of it had exploded in her mind when the spell was shattered.

"There is power here in this palace. I never knew— he kept me locked away from it."

Hexet did not point out to her that she had allowed herself to be locked away, had welcomed it. But her face was filled with the shame of that.

"I did it only because there were no more dragons. Because I was all alone. . . ."

Hexet leaned close to her. "There *are* dragons," he said softly. "I believe there are dragons." He looked up into her faded eyes. "I believe there are dragons here on Dacia. I have good reason to believe it." He saw a spark come alive, a germ of yearning and fire. "I believe, Queen Stephana, that if you will do as I say—now, today—I believe that you will see them."

News of the bear-creature that had killed two of Sardira's soldiers exploded into gossip that spun across the city like wildfire, increasing the number of dead soldiers tenfold and painting the bear tall as the palace. Tales spun from urchin to shopkeeper to brothel and tavern, then out along the streets. Soon no one in the city was ignorant of the killer bear that had been captured and would star in the stadium games, pitted against its own master, against bulls and the horse-sized lizards. The city, wild for the sight of blood, laid odds thirty to one, fifty to one, all in favor of the bear. Well before the stadium games began, the five gates to the stands were jammed with shouting commoners sucking on clay bottles of mithnon and sniffing cadacus or licking it from the backs of dirty hands. Small children came glaze-eyed, shouting for gore, and when the gates were thrown open the crowds stormed into the stands, the drunks and cadheads screaming and stamping, pushing their fellows off the stone bleachers onto the heads of others. Before the games began, more than a dozen citizens lay dead, ignored by their seething fellows, and others had crawled away injured.

The first game was a teaser, designed to heighten their lust to new frenzy.

A naked, bound prisoner was dragged into the center of the arena, a man jailed two months before for annoying a palace guard when he tried to deliver cabbages. He lay staring at the gate, shivering and exposed, as two dozen maddened, steel-spurred gamecocks, raised on a diet of raw meat, were dumped out of baskets onto his prone body. The crowd's cheering excited the roosters further.

Kiri could see through the arrow slits in the low stone wall below the seats as she moved beneath the stands, but she did not look. The victim's screams were enough, alone, to make her sick; that, and the crowd's insane shouting.

It was damp under the stands, and smelled of urine. She knew that, somewhere above her among the crowded benches, Garit watched the bloody games. So did a handful of rebel soldiers, though the bulk of the rebel forces had remained outside the gate, milling and shouting with the rabble that could not get in; they were more mobile out there, and might be of more use. Prince Tebriel was the first prisoner for whom the rebel armies had come out of hiding in force. He was perhaps the only prisoner for whom they would have shown themselves so openly. They had counted on reinforcements from other countries, time to arm more heavily before they declared open war. It was all happening too fast.

She approached the cages beneath the stands warily,

for Sardira's soldiers were thick around them, keeping the rabble back. They let a few street folk through, those wild with drugs and armed with sharp sticks to tease the captives. A horse screamed, and there was a deep bellowing that must be the bear. The crowd was so thick around the bars she could not see Tebriel. As she pushed her way through, she could see a herd of old, lame horses being driven out of a pen into the arena. They were followed by a spotted bull forced out with spears. It kept charging the fence, maddened from the cadacus it had been given.

Then, looking down through the cages, she saw the silver bear. It was sitting on its haunches, silent and still, watching the arena.

Had they given cadacus to the bear? Sometimes the drug produced rage, and sometimes lethargy. Had they drugged Tebriel? In humans, the cadacus stirred false power, making them foolhardy; then soon they would collapse into a depression of terror.

A knot of men forced her back from the bars, and one of them pinched her crudely. She flung away from him, her wound searing her with pain, then slipped into a crowd of laughing, drunken couples. She fought her way back to the cages, away from the pinching men, and grabbed up a stick as if to prod along with half a dozen others. She pressed against the bars, staring down though the row of cages, and could just see the great bear. She backed away when the caged black bull charged her, hitting the bars like an earthquake. The bull's tormentors jeered.

As she worked her way to the left toward the bear, she could see a dozen horse-sized brown lizards writhing beyond. In the last cage stood Tebriel chained to the wall, his leathers stained with blood. She began to push toward him, but five drunken boys blocked her, laughing, and one grabbed her arm. She kicked him in the leg, kneed him, and spun away, tunneling through the mob, ducking and shoving.

The prince stood with his back to her, watching the stadium, where, now, the spotted bull charged blood-hungry lizards among the bodies of the dying horses. Kiri watched the crowd. No one seemed interested in Tebriel; all were watching the bloody game. She whispered to him. He seemed glued to the spectacle of killing. When she spoke again, he turned.

His eyes were filled with fury; his face was drawn; his fists were clenched white. Such anger filled him that he did not recognize her at first. Then his eyes changed. He came to the bars to look down at her.

"Kiri! Oh . . ." His eyes searched hers, puzzled at the emotion that flared between them. He was tired, wounded, sick with the killing in the arena, straining to keep his head when he knew he might die soon.

"A man with red hair sent me," she said softly.

"Garit," he whispered. Then a flash of suspicion showed deep in his eyes. She reached to touch his hand.

A man glanced at her and turned away. A rag woman wandered by close to her and didn't look, one of Garit's trusted spies. Kiri made as if drunk, trying to throw up against the cage bars as a group of girls moved near.

When she and Tebriel seemed ignored again, she said, because she knew Garit would expect it, and to prove herself to Teb—but not because she needed proof, now, "What hangs on the walls of your palace?"

His eyes flared with interest. "Tapestries. They were bright once, but now they're ruined, maybe gone. Do you know what they showed?"

"Other worlds," she said, "that you had never seen."

He nodded.

"What color dress did your mother wear most?"

"Red. A red dress brighter than the flowers of the flame tree in her walled garden where she sat with us. Do you know the name of my first pony?"

"Linnet," she said. Their eyes held. The crowd surged around them. He turned away, pretending to watch the arena. She could see the scar on his arm, twisting a small, dark blemish that must be the mark of the dragon. Her own mark was where she could not decently show it. She wanted to tell him what she was. She felt shy and awkward. When the crowd had passed, she spoke softly, watching his leather-clad back. "You and Camery used to sit in the walled garden together."

He spun to face her, his face open now and eager. "*Camery!* It *was* Camery who had escaped from Vurbane. Where . . . ?"

"She will come soon. She is safe." Then, "Garit is in the stadium. He will help you. We will all help you. Our people . . ." She hardly breathed the words.

188

His own voice was so low she had to press her face to the bars to hear him. "The resistance . . . you are . . . ?"

She nodded, then backed away as the crowd pressed around them.

Beyond, in the arena, mounted soldiers were dragging away the carcasses of dead lizards and horses. Kiri caught the eye of the rag woman who had lingered, and nodded. The old woman faded into the crowd. She would pass the word to another, and so to another. It would reach Garit quickly through the milling crowds: *Tebriel! Yes, he is Tebriel.* And rescue plans would begin.

Had Garit had time to do more than organize archers to mount the outer stadium walls and shoot the animals that attacked Tebriel? Maybe mounted rebels would crash the gates. War in the stadium would erupt quickly, Kiri knew, into all-out war across the city. There was no way to prevent it.

More old, crippled horses had been turned in with the bulls. The carcasses dragged away would be divided among the crowds. That, too, she supposed was reason for the excitement. If they ate drugged meat, what was the difference?

Teb started to speak, but guards thronged around his gate. Three pushed inside to unchain him. She backed off at the first movement, but their eyes met and held; then she faded back into the crowd that was now shouting for the blood of the prince.

They stripped him nearly naked as the crowd stamped

and shouted. They prodded the bear until it roared and struck at its tormentors. They forced it into the arena, forced Teb in behind it. Would the bear, pain-maddened, drug-maddened, turn on its master? In the ring now were the bear and two bulls, a dozen lizards, a few horses still on their feet cowering at one end, and one young dragonbard stripped and weaponless, a chain dragging from his ankle. Kiri stared up at the stands hoping for a glimpse of Garit, then felt a hand on her arm. She spun, her knife raised—Summer stood close, staring past her toward the arena and Teb.

In the arena, Teb turned as if someone had spoken his name. Behind him the bulls pawed. He stared at Camery, their looks frozen—then he saw her alarm, turned fast as the bulls charged. He stood in front of one. It roared down on him. He stepped aside so it passed him. The two bulls charged one another, locking horns, sparring, forgetting Teb for a moment. The bear had risen over Teb—but only to protect him.

Camery's voice was choked. "I came too late. Oh, Kiri, it *is* Teb. The army—could we attack now? Where is Garit?" Her pale hair was hidden by a dirty scarf, her face smeared with soot. "Oh, what is Garit doing? Teb will be killed. We . . . Come on!" She grabbed Kiri's arm and pushed through the crowd toward the gate that led into the arena, her hand on her sword. Kiri started to follow, terrified, knowing this was not the way yet that they must help him quickly. But suddenly another power touched her, another knowledge. She grabbed Camery's arm and tripped her. Camery turned on her with fury.

"Wait," Kiri whispered. "Wait." Her thoughts were stirring with a power that made her tremble. She turned and stared up at the stands. . . .

She began to drag Camery toward the stairs that led up. Camery fought her at first, then began to run, her eyes wide with the strange, unbidden knowledge. Something was drawing them upward toward the top of the stands where the king's box rose—some power they could not resist.

Yet, behind them, Teb faced death.

He was a tiny figure now below them in the yawning arena. The spotted bull charged. The crowd roared; the iron gates heaved as resistance soldiers fought their way forward. Kiri battled the crowd upward with Camery, falling over feet, stepping on hands, until they reached the satin-draped royal box. They dove into a narrow space behind it.

It was dark behind the low wall of the box, and smelled musty. They could not see the arena, only hear the shouting, muffled by the two walls between which they crouched. Light came through the space above them, between the top of the wall and the satin-draped roof. Directly above them, they could see sky. Kiri didn't know why they had come, but she knew they had to be here. Power had called them. Power for them to seek and use . . . Power that could help Tebriel.

Kiri could hear Accacia's voice through the space

above the wall, then General Vurbane's. At the sound of his voice, Camery went pale and pulled her scarf farther over her face and hair and, kneeling, scraped up a handful of dirt to smear her face darker. Accacia's salmon-pink veil had caught across the top of the wall above them, where it ended some inches above Kiri's head.

Vurbane said in a flat voice, "Perhaps the bull will kill him. No, I will bet on the bear. Though it seems rather dull. Didn't they give it drugs?"

"It spit out the drugs," Accacia said. "It injured five men when they tried to force it."

Then Sardira's low voice, muffled by the wall. "It has been prodded and burned all morning. It is an extremely stupid bear."

"Yes. The creature seems to be defending the prisoner," Vurbane said. "I could have better entertainment in my own pasture."

"Wait," Accacia said, her scarf bobbing. "Patience, General. Wait until the lizards kill the bear; then the bulls will have the prince to themselves.

"Bets on that," said Vurbane lazily. "Bets . . . fifty to one . . . New bets, my dear."

"Ninety to one for the bull." Accacia laughed. Kiri could hear Roderica's laughter, too.

Camery pressed close to Kiri, her fists clenched. When she glanced at Kiri, her look was still puzzled. "A power to help him," she whispered. "The bard's power—try, Kiri." But already Kiri was trying with everything she knew to bring strength around Tebriel, a strength to increase his own.

"The bear," Vurbane shouted. "Chain the bear."

Suddenly they saw the king's black-sleeved hand lift above the wall as he signaled. The crowd stilled. Quiet spread as if time itself had frozen.

In the stillness, chains rattled.

Suddenly the silence was shattered with the crowd's wild shouting. *"Chain the bear . . . chain the bear . . ."*

The bear was roaring, its rising voice thundering. A man screamed.

"Kill it!" someone shouted from the box. "If you can't chain it, kill it!"

"Chain the prisoner!" a woman yelled. The bulls bellowed. The crowd started to stamp, shouting, *"Blood! Blood!"*

Kiri nudged Camery, then climbed up the rough-lumber wall, quickly past the opening and onto the canopy, Camery close behind, both hoping the noise of the crowd hid their commotion.

The satin-covered roof was usually filled with servants and pages who had climbed up secretly, but now it was deserted. Maybe they had been routed earlier. Lying flat on their stomachs, Kiri and Camery could see the arena clearly.

The black bull lay dead. The bear was standing on its hind legs swinging its bloody paws over three giant lizards that lay torn open at its feet. But the bear was bleeding, too, from a gash in its side. Teb crouched near the center pole covered with blood. The spotted bull moved toward him pawing, the steel tips on its horns catching the light. Camery's fists were white, her lips moving with her effort. Kiri fought harder. She watched the bull circle Teb shaking its metal horns, saw Teb rise. The bear moved to protect him, stood rearing over the bull so the bull backed away. But suddenly the bull staggered uncertainly, nearly fell—more than the bear had made it cower. Every creature in the arena cowered down except the bear. A fierce power touched the gaming field. Kiri gasped as she felt that power joining with her own, with Camery's, violent and strong.

Every creature in the arena was frozen still. Kiri and Camery were caught in a power much greater than their own, had become a part of that power that had stopped the killing. . . .

Camery touched her hand and pointed behind them. Someone in the box below them gasped. Kiri felt the power and saw the source of it approaching them.

Coming through the king's private gate were four soldiers carrying a litter chair. In the seat rode a thin, wrinkled old woman dressed in the royal purple and green, her skin like parchment, her wild white hair so thin her scalp showed through. Kiri had not glimpsed the queen in years. The soldiers carried her toward the royal box, but when she raised her hand they paused. She looked up directly at Kiri and Camery, and a force linked them that left Kiri breathless. This woman—

she had called them here. *She* was the source of the power. . . .

Below them the box was astir. "The *queen* has come. . . ."

"The queen? I don't believe . . ."

In the arena, the bull faltered and fell to its knees. Soldiers galloped in and prodded it. More lizards were released, but they, too, faltered. The force of the dark and the force of the light crashed around them. Kiri strained, heady with the power that linked her and the queen and Camery.

But soldiers were dragging Teb toward the center pole. *Fight them, Teb. Fight . . . we're with you. . . .* Her pulse raced; Camery's face swam; the queen's pale eyes seemed huge. Kiri saw the soldiers falter before they reached the pole, saw Teb spin, knocking soldiers to the ground, saw the bear grab the bull by the neck and shake it.

The bear had grown immense. It looked misty. What was happening? Shapes were dissolving, swirling. . . .

Something white like mist writhed in the arena, and the bear was gone; something gigantic and coiling, towering, a fog-thing growing denser, all pearl and silvery with light. A dragon shape—a dragon . . . and the dragon's shoulder was red with flowing blood. A pearl-colored dragon filled the arena, its wings spread to darken the stands. The crowd cowered, silent.

The naked, blood-covered prince gathered up his dragging chain and climbed painfully to the dragon's back. Nothing moved in all the stadium.

The dragon leaped into the sky suddenly, beating its wings across the stands so its wind tore at the cowering watchers. Kiri and Camery stared after it hungrily, pummeled by dragon wind.

There was no other sound but that wind.

The dragon swept away fast, until it was only a speck in the sky.

Then suddenly it was coming back, growing larger. But now there were more than one. *"Four,"* Kiri breathed. *"Four."*

Four dragons filled the sky, two white and two black, now so low over the stadium that the stands and arena were dark. Their wind tore at the crowd. Huge green eyes looked down. Open mouths flamed. Teb looked down between the white dragon's wings, laughing. Their wind was so strong that satin ripped from the king's box. A woman shrieked. The stands exploded in panic, the thunder of running, of stampeding and screaming, filled Kiri's ears.

One black dragon swept down so low his face was right above them, golden eyes blazing. Camery stared up, reached up to him.

Camery, he thundered in their minds. *Camery . . . soon . . . I searched for you. You are safe. Soon . . .* He banked, his wing sliding over them so Camery's hands stroked ebony feathers. He lifted, twisting, blazing upward to join his brother and sisters.

The dragons swept higher as stampeding crowds fought to get out the gates. Dragon wings shattered the light when they banked. They twisted, then soared into cloud, moved fast away from the stadium, grew smaller. . . .

They were gone. Gone.

Kiri stared up at the empty sky, yearning.

Nothing moved in the arena. A tableau of bloody bodies, a few bleeding horses crowded at one end. Dead bulls, but no bear. The thunder of running and screaming still came in waves. Kiri looked down at the queen.

The four soldiers still stood at attention bearing her litter chair, but the queen did not look back. She lay sprawled across the litter chair unnaturally twisted, with the king's jeweled knife through her heart.

CHAPTER

17

Kiri was not sure later how she and Camery managed to get out of the stadium, only that they kept fighting and pushing toward the nearest entry. They found themselves at last on an empty back street among the derelict buildings. Kiri's thoughts were filled with dragons, and with the sight of the poor murdered queen. She was shivering.

When they turned to look back toward the stadium, they saw only a few stragglers wandering; the crowd, once stampeded, had been quickly absorbed back into the city. On the road that approached the palace, they saw the long procession moving upward, green uniforms and yellow. The flash of salmon pink would be Accacia's dress.

"What did we do?" Kiri said. "What did we do back there? It was the queen's power—the poor dead queen." She stared at the empty sky. "Oh, the dragons, Camery. The dragons . . ."

Camery was crying. "Yes. Yes . . . He is Nightraider. . . . Oh, Kiri . . ." She dissolved into tears again.

Kiri watched her, glad for her but jealous, too. She couldn't help the icy loneliness that gripped her. She knew quite well she should be filled with joy that there were dragons. She was, only . . . to know there truly were dragons made her yearning so much more powerful.

Camery raised her tearstained face, saw Kiri's look, and put her arm around her. "There will be a dragon for you."

They sat quietly for some time. Camery said, "The queen died for what she did. She died for Teb."

"We didn't know what she was," Kiri said. "No one knew."

"Dragonbard. She had the blood of the bards. That was why he locked her away." Camery climbed onto a low broken wall, her grimy skirt blending with the stone. She pulled off the rag that covered her hair, and it spilled out golden. "Why did she come to the stadium? How did she know about Teb, what he really was? I can't forget her eyes. She knew about us."

"No one in the palace knew about us," Kiri said. "The animals knew. And Papa and Garit, and Marshy. Maybe she didn't know about us. Maybe she knew about Teb, and came there to save him. Then, when she sensed our power, she drew us there to the king's box, to help her."

"Maybe. But how did she know about Teb? And where is he now? Where have the dragons gone? Oh, Kiri, he was just a little boy the morning I watched him ride away a prisoner, his hands and feet tied. I thought he would die; I thought Sivich would kill him. And now—now he's riding dragons." She wiped away tears. "I can't wait to see him, to talk to him."

"I suppose he'll return without the dragons," Kiri said. "They would cover the city. Unless they can change into something small—tamer than a bear. They would be . . ." She stopped, stared at Camery, nearly choking. "Unless they can change . . . change into . . . Oh!" Her breath came sharply as the vision filled her mind.

"They're *not* horses," she breathed at last. "They never were horses. Two black stallions, two white mares. . . . No wonder Prince Tebmund's horses were so wonderful. No wonder they were allowed to roam free."

"Shape shifters," Camery said, her eyes alight. "Dragons . . . shape shifters. All of a sudden the whole world is different." She searched the clouds, the horizon. "Oh, Kiri, would they go to Gardel-Cloor?"

Kiri had been staring at the sky, too, praying they would return. She looked at Camery. "Oh, yes."

Camery slipped down from the wall and tied on her dirty scarf to cover her hair. They went quickly down through the ruins.

But they had hardly reached the bottom of the rubbled slope when the city exploded into shouting, the clang of weapons, galloping across cobbles as the king's soldiers pursued rebel forces. Camery drew the dagger from her boot, Kiri clutched her sword, and they moved in shadow into the city streets. Ahead, a band of the king's men, unhorsed, fought against baker and tinsmith and tavern regulars who had stepped from their roles as useless drunks and now wielded weapons stolen from the king's stores. The girls saw their own people attack and fall back into shadows, attack again, feinting, leading the king's troops into traps; they saw their own people fall. They were motioned on each time, and they ran.

Twice they were nearly trapped; once they played dead and were almost trampled by the king's mounted troops. They ran for Garit's street, dodging, racing. They reached the ruined tower and wrenched the door open, and wedged it shut from inside with a heavy timber.

It was only a small watchtower, so tight a space they elbowed each other when they knelt to dig in the rubble that littered the floor. Once they had pushed that into a heap, Kiri pressed herself against the stone wall as Camery raised the trapdoor.

Beneath were piles of arrows and five bows. Camery grabbed up two, and they took all the arrows they could carry, letting the door down silently. As they climbed the narrow spiral that led to the top, Kiri thought of Gram, with the fighting maybe raging close below the castle. But Gram would go up into the palace kitchens with the servants, as they had always planned. No one would notice one more woman; no one would care. The palace would likely be safest. Gram knew it well enough to get through into cave rooms beneath the mountain, and she knew how to find the tunnels that led out to the other side where the mountain was wild and unpeopled. They reached the broken top of the tower and crouched low beneath its jagged stone parapet. Below them were seven king's horsemen pinioning three resistance soldiers against a tavern wall. Both girls drew arrow and took aim.

The four dragons churned close to one another in the heaving sea, the waters pink with Seastrider's blood, and with Teb's. He treaded water beside her as she wallowed to let the sea wash her wounded shoulder; the salt stung like fire, but it would help to heal the torn flesh.

They remained resting in the rough sea for some time; then the dragons reared up out of the waves, shattering water with their beating wings as they rose, heading for the black mountain above the palace, Seastrider's flight slow and painful. Below them as they flew, clashes of yellow and green marked the soldiers of the dark forces locked in battle with the rebel armies. They could see a pincer movement where two armies of king's soldiers had cornered a small band. Then, ahead of Teb, Windcaller banked away to the north, and Nightraider and Starpounder followed.

Far out on the sea, five ships were heading for Dacia. The three dragons circled them, diving low to see whose troops they carried. Dragons were no longer a secret; everyone would know soon. They screamed their fury at sight of Quazelzeg's dark troops, and dove. Those troops would never see land. Teb and Seastrider beat in limping flight for the black mountain.

She came down stumbling onto the far side of the peak, and wound herself in between jutting boulders and twisted trees until she seemed no more than a white stone ridge. The blood had ceased to flow so hard, was only oozing now, but it was a large wound, and ragged. Teb slid down from her back. When she had settled and seemed to rest easy, he turned to leave.

"I do not like you going alone, Tebriel."

"And I do not like leaving you wounded. The dark is too strong. It will be eager to get at you. You must promise to fly at once if they come here." He hugged her pearly neck and laid his head against her cheek. "We must have the lyre. The power that helped us in the stadium is gone."

"She is dead," Seastrider said. "The queen is dead." She stared at Teb. "The power that freed us, freed me from the bear shape, is gone." She sighed.

He nodded, thinking of the frail queen.

"And the dark has increased *its* power," Seastrider said. "You must take care, Tebriel."

Teb left her, not looking back. The dark's power might be stronger, and laced with hatred of the dragons, but there were three bards now. And he sensed more. They would bring their powers stronger, they would beat the dark as, today, they had stifled it in the stadium.

He thought of Queen Stephana, willingly made prisoner, and could not imagine a bard turning her back on everything she truly was. Loneliness, he thought. She had believed there were no more dragons. She hadn't tried very hard to find out. . . .

His mother had tried. She had gone searching in spite of the pain it had caused to leave her family. To be a bard held a commitment to others.

Well, Queen Stephana had fulfilled her commitment today—her last living act.

He made his way up over the ridge, crouching low so his silhouette would not be seen against the setting sun, and started down the other side, above the black spires of the palace, keeping to shelter near rock outcroppings and small trees, moving in the mountain's shadow. When he found a sharp black stone that fit his hand, he took it for a weapon.

He hoped Kiri's Gram would be there in the cottage below the palace. He remembered her eager interest, watching the four horses. He was naked, all but a breechcloth. He needed clothes and a weapon. Maybe she could manage a disguise that would take him safely through the palace. His chambers would be watched; she was the only person he could go to. If Kiri trusted her, then so could he.

He followed the black boulders that had stacked themselves down the side of the mountain, until he came to the south end of the palace above the servants' quarters and the kitchens. He slipped by these buildings quickly and saw no one, though he could hear excited voices inside and sharp commands. He could hear a stir from the far stable, too, the echo of a horse's scream, the thin sound of hooves pounding as, he supposed, more troops were readied. He had skirted the palace at last. He slipped over the wall where grapevines grew in an untended garden, and was soon pressed against the door of the cottage he had seen Kiri enter, knocking with soft, urgent blows.

The old woman opened the door at once as if she had been waiting for someone, then drew back with a gasp. Then she looked hard at his face, saw who he was, and pulled him inside. Her blue eyes were as bright as he remembered from that morning on the training field when they had seemed to spark with her admiration of the horses.

"I am . . . Prince Tebmund."

"I can see that, even without your fine clothes. How did you come here? What is happening down there? The battles . . ."

"The rebels are fighting. You are Kiri's grandmother?"

She nodded. "You may call me Gram, as she does. Where is she?"

"I don't know. She was in the stadium."

"You were there . . . ?"

"I was part of the games."

"The gossip was right, then. And now . . ." She glanced out the little window. "Now . . ."

"Now the rebellion has begun," he finished for her.

"Then likely Kiri is fighting in the streets," she said

stoically, but he could see the fear in her eyes. Then she fixed a look on him. "And why do you come here?"

"Do you know of the Ivory Lyre?"

Her eyes grew wary.

He studied her, tried to see beyond that sudden hood of secrecy. "Only the Ivory Lyre of Bayzun can help us now. Only it can help the rebel forces. Do you side with the rebel forces? Or with the dark? Do you side against your own granddaughter?"

She studied him with care. A heavy silence touched the room, and her eyes burned a challenge. "Kiri spoke of a lyre. What do you want with it?"

"I can bring its power."

"Only a bard can do that."

He stared at her.

"How am I to believe you?" she said softly.

"If I were of the dark, and I knew about the lyre, I would force its location from the king and destroy it. Likely the dark does not know—yet."

She sighed. "Kiri overheard you make a spell to charm the information from Accacia." She shook her head. "The Ivory Lyre of Bayzun. The power of the ancient dragon."

"So, your Kiri gathers information."

"Perhaps. But she did not hear where the lyre is. Accacia didn't tell you that. Why do you come *here* looking for it? What makes you think I would know?"

"I don't think you know. But I think you will help me. I saw the way you watched my horses. I need clothes, Gram. A weapon better than this stone. I need any help you can give—if you are for the rebels."

She went to a cupboard and rummaged among clothes, then drew forth a full skirt of brown hearthspun and a gray linen smock. "You will have to go barefoot; my shoes won't fit, nor will Kiri's. You will not be able to fasten the skirt, but you can tie the belt. The smock will be tight in the shoulders."

He dressed quickly and found the skirt hit him at mid-calf. The loose smock covered him well enough, and he tied over his head the scarf she offered. She adjusted it so it covered more of his face. "We will go the back way."

"We?"

"I will lead you. Unless you are more familiar with the palace than I. You will be less suspect as one of a pair of old women than going alone. You must walk like a woman, and keep your face down."

"The upper treasure room first, the one near the parapet."

She nodded. "That stone weapon of yours could break a lock, I suppose." She took from a cupboard a finely made sword, in a scabbard. He buckled the scabbard on, then tied over it the apron she handed him, grinning at her.

"You are very resourceful."

She didn't answer but led him out and along the path to the south. She carried only a lantern, unlit. "Do try to bend over, Prince Tebmund. And take smaller steps. No old woman has that kind of stride."

Below them in the streets the fighting had moved

to the north and eastward toward the harbor. When he turned to look back, toward the sea in the north, he could see no movement in the sky there; nor could he see any ships. Just down the hill, half a dozen bodies sprawled. A band of riderless horses galloped up the road toward the palace, reins and stirrups flying.

Gram entered through a small gate in the palace wall. They passed the servants' quarters, then climbed a narrow stair in darkness, holding hands. They went along an upper passage, Gram careful and certain. "Here," she said, "this is the door." He reached out, could feel the oak and the crossed metal strapping. Behind them, they heard footsteps, then saw a light down the hall. They moved away, pressing into a niche beside a cupboard. A soldier passed them swinging his lantern, jingling keys.

It was the treasure room door the soldier opened. His light shone in on barrels and crates and a scattering of gold goblets and bowls. Teb hit him on the head with the stone. He dropped at their feet. Teb pocketed his keys and dragged him inside, then stood surveying the chamber.

There was no sense of bright power here, as there had once been outside the door. The barrels and crates would take all night to open and the effort turn out useless. Teb locked the door and they went on, winding through black passages by Gram's sense of the palace until at last she had to stop and strike flint to light her lantern. A quarter hour later, they descended a narrow stair, going steeply down. The air felt damp and smelled of mold. They went along a cleft in the mountain where no pretense had been made to smooth the walls.

When they came to a metal-clad door, Teb tried the five keys but none would turn. Gram removed a clasp from her hair and, as he held the lantern, she poked it into the lock, twisting delicately. He had to laugh. A dragon would have melted the lock with one breath, but now he had only Gram, trying to pick it with a trinket of tin.

CHAPTER

18

The setting sun stained the sky with blood, mirroring the blood in Dacia's streets, and still the royal armies wheeled after rebels that struck from behind, then vanished to strike again. The king's frustrated troops took as prisoners the confused townsfolk they found cowering in corners and abandoned shops, unwilling to fight for either side. These were herded into makeshift cells, and the doors and windows were nailed shut.

In some quarters the rebel army tried to force the uncertain townsfolk to stand ground against the king, but found only a useless, cowering lot on their hands. On a corner near the quays, Garit's forty raiders fled from a green-clad battalion and vanished, then silently attacked from behind. They confiscated the dead soldiers' uniforms and pulled them on, and took the uninjured horses and the weapons. So a new king's band rode through Dacia, joining other king's soldiers, then turning on them with the king's own swords. It was the only attack they could master now, for in many quarters of the city the dark forces were winning.

But the dark leaders got no new reinforcements from the sea as they had expected. No boat stirred the waters, and still the sky was patrolled by the three dragons.

Atop the stone watchtower, Kiri and Camery killed five horsemen, and saw them relieved of their yellow tunics and their weapons and wandering mounts. The false army grew slowly against the larger forces of the dark. But the dark lusted for battle and took strength from seeing men die.

In the back of the barrelwright's storeroom behind stacks of oak timbers and lathes, children kept the stew pot boiling, dished up meals and tended wounds. There were too many wounded and not enough blankets or bandages. In the chandler's, weapons were passed out the back door. In the sleeping loft of a tavern, four young girls picked off the king's soldiers with heavy slingshots and sharp stones. Along the coast the great cats massed, charging into side streets to cripple and stampede the king's horses and kill the fallen riders with quick, bone-crushing skill.

Teb and Gram could hear the lock's insides move, but they couldn't get it open with her hair clasp. At last he took the stone to it, pounding until it gave way with a loud snap, scattering its parts across the stone floor. He pulled the door open; Gram held the lamp high.

The cave had a tall ceiling and was so deep the light

melted away before it reached the back. The floor could not be seen for the piles of silver and gold that reflected the guttering light. There were shields and caskets, pitchers and plateware and urns and saddlery, gold bedposts and chamber pots and tall, gold-crusted chairs with laddered backs. Casks and chests stood open, with jewels spilling to the floor.

But Teb surveyed the treasure room with disappointment. There was no sense of the lyre here, no hint of the magic he had felt in the palace above. Then Gram caught her breath sharply and he spun, sword drawn.

Accacia stood in the doorway flanked by four green-clad soldiers, their blades catching the light. Teb flung the lamp at them and spilled fire over one, struck another with a blow that sent him rolling among the treasure, moaning. He faced the other two crouching, and caught a glimpse of Gram snatching up something bright from the treasure heap. He countered the two blades, trying not to be backed into the tangle of treasure and tripped, fighting close and hard with short jabs. Soon one soldier was down, but the other had drawn a knife and ducked under Teb's blows—then he went down suddenly, his head lolling against his shoulder. Gram stood over him, the hilt of a gold ax tight in her two thin hands. Accacia snatched up his fallen blade and swung. Teb tripped her, forced the blade from her, and forced her down with his knee. She glowered up at him as he pulled off the heavy cord that bound her hair.

"Tie her hands, Gram."

Gram tied her hands roughly, the two scowling at each other. There was no love between these two. Accacia's eyes were hard, her mouth set in a scowl.

Teb looked her over coldly. "Why did you come here? Why did you follow us?"

She stared at him, mute and furious.

"You came because you knew I would search for the lyre," he said more gently. "But why didn't you just tell the king, let him deal with me?"

Her look remained defiant, but he saw a flash of some deeper anger, too.

"You are angry with the king," he said softly, testing her. "The king has kindled such fury in you—" He saw her look grow uncertain and felt a rising strength in himself. "You came here to spite the king," he said, and saw his guess was the truth. "You followed me, Accacia, hoping . . . to discover me with the lyre." Yes, he saw the truth in her eyes.

"To find you with it," she said, "take you captive and present you to the king. *Show* the king . . . show him. . . ."

"He was cruel to you."

"He was furious. He thought *I* told the queen that you were captive in the stadium. I *told* him it was Roderica, but then Roderica, the little traitor—" She paused, scowling.

"Go on, tell me all of it." There seemed no need to charm her now; her anger made her speak, spilling hatred.

"I *told* him it was Roderica. I know her—everything for the queen. Sardira grabbed Roderica's arm to keep her from running out of the stadium when . . . when the dragons—" She swallowed, pale with fear at that memory. "Roderica denied telling the queen you were captive. But who else could have?" Her eyes blazed with hatred. "But Roderica told Sardira something else. She told him you made me speak about the Ivory Lyre. She said she heard it all. I don't remember," Accacia said, staring at him with fury.

"Who told the queen I was captive?"

"I don't know! If not Roderica, who would? It would take a terrible power on the queen's part to make the king's servants obey her. To make them carry her to the stadium. His orders were that she never leave the palace." She swallowed again and her eyes showed pain. "It would take a terrifying power to do . . . what she did."

Teb smiled. It was interesting to see something really touch her, frighten and confuse that smug little ego.

"It was the queen who saved you," she said in a small, lost voice. But her look at him was of hatred.

"The queen didn't know about the lyre?" he asked, knowing she could not have, not until the spell was broken.

"She didn't know. That was partly why he kept her locked up . . . away from the places that hid the lyre, away from the tablet that told about it."

"And where is the tablet?"

"In his chambers, behind a panel in the wall." Her eyes blazed. "What difference does it make now if I tell? What difference? He has already called me a traitor and told me to leave the palace."

"So you came to find me with the lyre, to take me captive and deliver me to him, to soothe his fury."

"Yes. But it doesn't matter. If I don't take you to him, he will find you. He will kill you anyway."

"Where is the lyre now? Where has he hidden it?"

"I don't know."

He forced the spell again. "Where is the lyre? You know you will have to tell me."

She glared back at him, then slowly her face grew docile, her eyes dulled. "The lyre is in the queen's chambers, where her dead body lies."

"Why would he take it there?"

"A joke, his cruel joke . . . that he take it to her, now that she could no longer use it. He kept it secret for so many years, but now . . . now he has given it to her."

He took her hands, twisting her tied wrists so she had to follow him. "You are coming with us to search for it. If you cause a problem I will kill you."

He pushed her toward the passage. As she passed Gram, her look at the old woman was cruel and puzzling. They went quickly up the passage, then up a narrow stair rising steeply into the heart of the mountain, then a low-roofed passage—not the one he had used to visit the queen. They joined that passage, but there was no sense of the lyre near the queen's door. Teb approached cautiously with drawn sword, forcing Accacia ahead.

"You will see the queen," she said, "lying there waiting to be buried."

"I have seen dead people before." Still there was no sense of the lyre, no sense of bright magic. He spun Accacia around to face him. "Is it a trick? You will die first if this is a trap."

She looked at him steadily. "The lyre is there, in her chamber, secured in a locked safe beneath her bed."

He forced her on, then saw the door was ajar and drew back. Too late. Soldiers surrounded them.

Teb flung Accacia aside, parrying blows, but there were too many, and the power of the un-men pressed at him, weakening him, striking him with sudden confusion. Perhaps they had confused him all along, led him here. It was a short battle and one-sided, two dozen blades and the power of the dark sending him sprawling, bleeding from a dozen wounds. Before him, beside the queen's bed, watching coldly, stood King Sardira, Captain Leskrank, and General Vurbane. They stared with icy amusement as Teb was led in to them defeated, his woman's skirts flapping around his ankles.

He looked back at them steadily, devoid of power, wishing mightily for Seastrider—as bear, as wolf—and realized how much he had grown to depend on her. Then, glancing at the bed, he was riven with shock.

There lay the little, thin body of the queen, brutally twisted across the satin as if the pain of her death still gripped her, the jeweled knife still protruding from her chest. The sight of her shocked Teb profoundly, that they had not arranged her in peace with her hands crossed, or even removed the knife or closed her eyes.

The soldiers bound him and Gram. They left Accacia's hands tied.

She fought in a rage, swearing at the king. "You told me if I brought him here, you told me—"

King Sardira smiled coldly. "Never believe the word of an angry king, my dear Accacia. You will find no forgiveness for what you did."

They were forced down passages and narrow stairs, beyond the passage to the treasure room, then at last through another door, into a long, rough fissure in the mountain that contained a line of empty cells, the soldiers' lamplight catching at the heavy bars.

They were locked there, each to a cell, but not adjoining ones. The lamps showed the king's lined face sharply. Teb stared at the uncertainty that showed for a moment in those dark eyes; then the king's look went shuttered and cold.

The line of soldiers was filing out to where the unmen waited in the passage beyond. The king still paused, staring at Teb.

"You will not leave me here, King Sardira," Teb

217

said softly. "If our people win, and you have killed me, your own life will be forfeit. They will know—the dragons will know. If the dark should win, you will need me then. Only I can use the lyre to drive the dark back and save you. Don't ever imagine, King Sardira, that the dark will leave you free. They know, now, what that power was that kept them from conquering you. Roderica confessed it all, in the stadium box.

"They will find the lyre now, King Sardira. You will have no protection, unless I am here to help, to use its power against them."

The king stared at him openly for a moment, his eyes questioning. Then he moved on through the heavy door behind the last soldier. The door was pushed to so the light died and was locked with a dull clang. The darkness was so complete Teb could not see the bars to which he clung. He stood trying to memorize the exact distance between himself and Gram, between him and Accacia, between himself and the door. It was the kind of cell where one did not expect to be freed except by death.

CHAPTER

19

Smothered by the darkness, Teb tried to feel some hint of the lyre from somewhere. He was blinded by blackness, could not move beyond bars. Even Seastrider's voice did not reach him. His very sense of time seemed warped, so he didn't know if it was still night. The sun had been low when he had left Seastrider on the mountain, the shadow of the mountain itself stretched long across the city when he and Gram had made their way into the palace. He reached out for the lyre's power and could feel nothing.

But it was there, somewhere in the labyrinth of the dark palace caves. Somewhere giant lizards guarded the Ivory Lyre of Bayzun, and he meant to know where.

Maybe Accacia knew, after all.

He began to question her, weaving his questions slowly, taking his time. She remained silent. He could not see or touch her to make the job easier.

At last she stirred in the darkness with a little rustling sound, and laughed. "Do you really think I would tell you anything, after you got me locked in this cell?"

"If you will tell me where the lyre of Bayzun is hidden, maybe I can get us out of here."

"What difference would it make to know where it is? If you don't have it, how could you use it? What could it do anyway against iron bars?"

"Did you believe in dragons before you saw them? Did you believe in the power of bards? The power of the queen?"

She was silent.

"If the dark wins the last battle, Accacia—if the dark were to rule Dacia—do you still think you would become a part of their court? Did you see any special favors when they took us captive in the queen's chambers?"

"They will come to get me. Once Sardira's temper cools, he will. They will not let you out, Prince Tebmund. Nor will they release my grandmother, not until they shovel out your bones."

Teb stared through the blackness. Her grandmother?

But of course, he should have known that. Hadn't Accacia told him? She seemed to have told him all about her life. He had not been paying attention. Their two mothers, Accacia's and Kiri's—they had been sisters. But she was trying to lead him away from talk of the lyre. Did she fear the lyre so much?

"Are the lizards all dead, Accacia? Did they all die in the stadium? Or do some still guard the lyre? Where, Accacia? Where do the lizards now gather?" She sighed, and he heard the faint rustle of her skirt again. "Where, Accacia? Where are the lizards?"

"In the sea vault."

"Where is the sea vault?"

"Beneath the mountain where it touches the sea on the far side. Sardira hardly ever opens the passage to the sunken cave. There is gold there, and he keeps lizards on the rocks around the cave and in the passages leading to it."

"How many passages? Where do they begin?"

"One in the sea. One from near the treasure chamber you forced open. That is the one Sardira uses."

"How close are we to the sea vault?"

She sighed and was silent for a few minutes, as if thinking over the lay of the passages. "Not far, I suppose. I imagine this cave isn't far from the southern sea cliffs."

He let the power ease away. All three of them were silent with their own thoughts. He lay down on the cool stone floor of his cell, tired suddenly but his mind alive with new hope. Beneath the mountain where it touched the sea, a passage to a sunken cave . . . He stretched his body long across the stone and felt his tension ease, then reached with his thoughts, toward Seastrider.

Within the warring city, within the broken tower, Kiri curled tighter against the stone parapet in fitful sleep, waking each time there was a sound from the street, or when Camery, standing guard, moved quickly to take aim. Kiri would jerk awake, then drop into sleep again, exhausted. Twice when Camery nudged her she was up at once, bow taut, her whole being keyed to sudden action. Then when the danger passed she dropped down to sleep hardly knowing she had stirred. Yet while her mind and body were tuned so tight to war, something within her dreamed of peace. She saw this war as a tiny, insane space in time. She saw all life suddenly and stupidly seeking to destroy itself, and woke angry that there was fighting at all.

But then she woke fully, her mind clearer. It was not all life that was seeking destruction. It was the un-life, the dark evil of the un-men, that sought to destroy the precious gift of life that all human blood and that of the many animals shared. The dark had made those dreams.

She thought of tired rebel soldiers sleeping hidden all over the city, nervous and edgy, waiting for dawn to begin again the terrible battle, and wondered if they had dreamed the same, and shivered. The dark knew it was not easy to fight at night, too easy to kill your own people. Night was a nervous truce breached often enough so guards stood at every shelter. Now the dark had breached that truce in a new and hideous way. She saw Camery yawning and rose to take the bow from her hands.

There should have been no new boats docking at the quays, for the three dragons had swamped and sunk every boatload of dark soldiers that moved anywhere in the northerly seas. But well to the south, unlighted boats clung to the black sea close beneath the cliffs of Edosta. They put in silently to Dacia, and the four heavy boats spewed forth horses and troops, the soldiers pulling dark capes over their yellow tunics. The horses had been silenced with wrapped bits and padded shoes. As dawn touched the seam of sky and sea far in the east, these warriors entered the city.

On the mountain, Seastrider woke. She lifted her head. Her long muscles tightened and expanded with sudden nerves. She stared up at the black sky, her unease making her shudder all through her long, gleaming body. In her mind she saw Tebriel, where he was held in a dark, close place. She twisted and thrashed, trying to see where, exactly where. This was unclear, but his message of a cave and passage touching the sea was vivid. She slipped out from beneath the trees, her wound making her stiff and slow, and pulled herself up toward the crest of the mountain.

Soon she lay along the crest staring over at the pale wash of the distant sea and the black jumble of the war-torn city unrelieved by any light. She gazed down at the palace, dark and still. She rumbled once deep in her throat, then turned back to examine the mountain again, for it was there, deep within, that she felt the sense of Teb.

She laid her head down along the mountain, crawling and scenting like a hunting snake, her tongue slipping in and out, her head hugging stone and earth and twisting one way, then the other, as she sought down along the mountain's wild reaches. Her newly forming scar tissue loosened, her hurt muscles warmed and eased until she moved more freely. She scented the inner shapes of the mountain, its caves and passages and the turnings of its rocky coast.

Well past midnight, as a group of king's soldiers slept inside a tavern with the door barricaded and two of their comrades standing guard, a shadow slipped silently across the cobbles, its tail lashing. It killed the guards. Soon five great cats climbed the stone building, from shed roof to window ledge, then pushed through the shutters into the dark rooms.

All five returned the same way, jumping down to the empty street, leaving dead soldiers behind. So the great cats prowled the war-torn city, five here, three there, seven, a great tom alone—all taking their toll, then vanishing. But suddenly they heard two mounted battalions coming softly along the street on padded hooves. As the battalions appeared, silhouetted against the dawn, the great cats slipped into cottages and shops to warn Garit's troops. Men rose, armed, and slipped out into the dawn's shadows.

In the tower, Kiri woke Camery as a great cat lingered on the stair. The two archers crouched ready. A thin seam of dawn's light shone at their backs. Soon came the soft *hush, hush* of rag-shod hooves along the cobbles. All over the city, rebel soldiers moved closer to the approaching riders, and in the tower Kiri and Camery held steady, their bows taut.

At the cry of "Redbull," the rebels struck, swordsmen and cats and spear throwers leaping out of cover to panic the long line of horses; mounts reared and spun, swords rang against swinging metal; the archers aimed high to pick off mounted men above their own comrades. Great cats leaped and brought down riders. As uniformed riders fell, rebels snatched up their weapons, caught their horses, and tore the yellow and green tunics off them. But too late they heard the racket of hooves, and four more battalions pounded in to block the surrounding streets, green-clad warriors fresh from sleep in the palace and mounted on fresh horses. They pounded into the melee, cutting and slashing. Kiri fired and fired again, she and Camery back to back. Then Kiri glanced up at the mountain and froze.

The great ridge of the black mountain had turned white. It was moving, gleaming in the rising dawn like silver and pearl as coils of the dragon's body caught and turned the light. Kiri pulled her gaze away, taking aim, firing, but longed to look again. The king's soldiers charged the tower, and she choked back a cry as they battered at the door with huge timbers. Her eyes met Camery's. They put aside their bows, drew swords, and waited at the top of the stairs. The pounding shook the tower so hard Kiri thought the stone would crumble. The door crashed in, she heard Elmmira's angry scream, then she was dodging the sword of the first soldier; she struck deep beneath his ribs and he went down. The next fell to Camery's sword; the next up the stairs lost his footing dodging Kiri's sword and fell onto his mates. Kiri and Camery finished them where they thrashed in a bloody tangle.

At the bottom of the stairs they found Elmmira with her teeth in a soldier's throat. They ran directly out into the battle, grabbed the first riderless horses they came to, and piled aboard, Elmmira leaping beside them. Kiri's frightened mare reared, then ran, leaping bodies, dodging battling men, pounding toward the mountain. There was power on the mountain, the power of the dragon, a power that could save Dacia. Where was Tebriel? Were he and the white dragon so badly hurt that they could not attack? Where were the other dragons?

In the blackness of his cell, Teb felt the sense of Seastrider touch him, then subside. He lay thinking of the sea vault, imagining the lyre there, making a picture in his mind of it for Seastrider; but he was frantic to be free, and soon he rose and began to feel along the base of the bars where they were set into mortar between the stones that formed the floor. Surely the mortar must be ancient, surely it must have a weak spot.

"Gram, if I could find a place to dig, do you still have your hair clip? Could you rip your skirt into a cord to tie to it and throw it to me?"

To his left, Accacia snorted. But on his right, in the blackness, Gram chuckled. "Yes, the clip . . ." Then the sound of ripping. "Here it comes."

A clink hit the bars; he heard the clip drop. He felt around his feet and through the bars, but couldn't find it. "It's gone too far outside. Try again."

It took Gram nine throws, aiming toward his voice, before the metal clasp fell in between the bars, so close it grazed his foot. He grabbed it up and knelt again to examine the floor of his cell, his fingers touching the mortar as delicately as an otter's paws would examine the sea floor.

Each time he found a tiny crack, he worked at it with the metal. But the mortar was hard; he could not break away so much as a chip. Soon he grew disgusted with the frail trinket and was about to throw it away when he came to a corner where the mortar was rough and crumbling.

The jagged rocks along the cliff tore at Seastrider as she searched for a way in toward Teb. She sensed the hollowness of caves. At last she found the opening to a tangle of caves that she knew, by the echoes, went far back into the mountain. She could sense Teb, sense his stubborn hope, and that kept her seeking. She moved deep in, not liking to be underground. But she sensed something else ahead of her, the hint of a bright and powerful magic. She pushed forward eagerly.

From above her on the mountain she heard the screams of dragons. The others had returned. She felt the vibrations of their bodies as they settled among the trees and boulders; then came a cry loud enough to crack the mountain right through. It was Nightraider, bugling. Only one thing made a dragon bugle. Nightraider had sensed his bard. The commotion was terrible and wonderful. Seastrider wanted to pull out of the caves and look, but she would not leave Teb. She sucked in fresh air and moved deeper in. She could see Teb in vision, stubbornly digging at the floor with a puny bit of metal, brushing the mortar away with his hands.

Kiri clung to the side of the mountain staring up, frozen with wonder at the sight above her as the great black dragon reared into the sky, bugling. Beside her Camery stared, too, her cheeks flaming and her eyes huge.

They had released their horses at the foot of the cliff where the climbing grew steep, pulled the saddles and bridles from the poor blowing beasts and sent them wandering away. Now, above them, the black dragon was a turbulence of dark coils, his wings snapping over the edge of the cliff, a huge clawed foot sliding over a boulder. Then the dragon's head was so close they could feel his hot breath, as he stared down at Camery, his eyes yellow and luminous. She looked up at him, then laughed out loud, and struggled upward fighting to get to him. He bugled again, then reached down.

His great mouth came over Camery so wide open they could see every knife-long fang. Camery looked up unafraid. He took her between his jaws with infinite gentleness. She pulled herself in, clinging to his ivory teeth, and he lifted her and set her on his back between his spreading wings. There Camery clung to him, her arms trying to circle his neck, and her bright hair spilling across his black scales.

As he gathered himself to leap skyward, she sat up straight on his back, clutching at the scallops of mane along his neck, pressing her booted legs tight to his sides. He lifted into the dawn.

Kiri watched them soar over the mountain. She could still feel the wind of the dragon's wings across her upturned face. The stone beneath her hands felt lifeless. She was only a small, earthbound creature.

But then the knowledge that there *were* dragons overrode all else. There were dragons again on Tirror. Her pleasure in Camery's freedom filled her soul. She began to climb again, up to where the other dragons waited.

CHAPTER
20

Teb dug with the clasp, the mortar dust filling his nose. The darkness pressed at him, making him want to batter mindlessly at his prison. The bar was slowly loosening; already he could wiggle it. He tried to keep the sense of Seastrider close, but even that was not constant. Sometimes he thought he heard rumbling over the scraping of mortar, but when he paused to listen he wasn't sure.

Soon the sound came louder; he felt Seastrider close as she battered against stone so hard he could hear the mountain rumble. Hot tears welled in his eyes. She was tearing at the mountain to reach him. He dug harder at the stubborn mortar.

She could hear the echo of emptiness behind the wall she battered, ramming it with her sides and with her horns. Though the cave was huge, this wall was not thick, and at last it gave way. But Teb was not there inside the big echoing space. She listened and could just hear faint tapping and scraping. He was in another cave beyond this one. She tore at the new wall, while above her on the mountain Kiri stood between dragons.

They pushed their noses at Kiri. She scratched Starpounder's black forehead. They were watching the city, and suddenly Starpounder drew away, then leaped skyward as a small band of king's soldiers rode out from the palace stables down along the curving road. Kiri watched the black dragon dive on them spitting flame, scattering the horses, dragging the men from their saddles. She watched Starpounder kill the soldiers and chase the horses away. Beside her Windcaller rose to attack another band near the river, her wings catching the sun with white light. Both dragons sped over the city slashing and ripping, but avoiding their own troops. Kiri saw Nightraider join them with Camery astride, her sword flashing. Moments later, Starpounder banked and returned to the mountain, sliding down the wind, his wings grazing her as he came to rest, nudging her until she leaped to his back.

He did not join the others over the city; he circled the mountain, then dropped low along its southern cliffs. She ducked as he glided into the big, echoing cave. Inside, far back, she could see Seastrider's pale shape battering at the cave wall. The next instant they were beside her in a shower of rock, as Starpounder, too, attacked the mountain. Kiri slid down, drew her sword and began to dig beside them, hacking at earth and stone.

Teb could hear them digging, could hear metal striking stone as he gouged at the flaking mortar. Accacia and Gram were quiet. As he forced his shoulder at the bar again, it broke away at the bottom so he fell half out of his cage. One more shove and he was out, still clutching the little hair clip. He ran in blackness toward the sound of digging, slammed into the wall, felt it trembling. Metal rang, thuds like stones falling. Then Seastrider's voice, "Stand back, Tebriel. The stone will bounce and roll."

He backed away, into bars, felt Gram's hand on his arm. "What is happening? Is it the dragons?"

"Yes, the dragons, Gram. Will you be afraid?"

She squeezed his hand and laughed. "Excited. Awed."

They heard stone fall, a dragon roared, thunder shook the mountain and boulders were tumbling in, the light so bright. Then Seastrider's face filled the hole, her green eyes on Teb, her white nose pushing at him. He was only vaguely aware of Kiri crowded against the wall sheathing her battered sword, for his arms were around Seastrider's neck, squeezing so hard she belched flame.

It was flame that freed Accacia and Gram as Seastrider's breath cut away the bars. Teb thought of leaving Accacia there, but he could not. He did leave her to climb out of the fissure alone, as he and Gram lifted into the sky between Seastrider's white wings and Kiri clung to Starpounder. As they dropped low over the sea along the cliff, they could see a tunnel well beneath the water. And now guard lizards began to appear on the mountain, slithering out of every crevice, snarling and hissing up at them.

The battle was quickly fought, the two dragons killing the lizards like a fox in a nest of mice, tossing them into the waves. If there were others, they had fled back into the cracks of the mountain. The riders slid down. Teb took Kiri's hand.

"Can you swim? Can you dive deep?"

"I can swim. I never tried to dive for long."

"I'll show you." He stripped off the brown skirt and tunic.

"They're Gram's," she said, laughing.

Teb chose two heavy stones. "Pull in your breath and hold it, relaxed and slow. Hold as long as you can, then let it out. Do that five times. Each time you will be able to hold longer. Then take the last breath, clasp the stone to you, and jump in. Let your breath out a little at a time under water. When you are ready to come up, drop the stone and kick."

Kiri pulled off her skirt and boots, modestly leaving her tunic on, and followed his lead down into the sea, her last breath so deep she thought her lungs would burst. She was terrified there would be more lizards. She and Teb dropped fast under the weight of the stones, the undersea all glowing with green light. Deep down they grabbed for the tunnel wall and pulled themselves in.

Not far inside the tunnel shone a metal door set into the mountain. Teb smashed at the lock with his stone. Kiri took a turn, but her need for air was getting uncomfortable. Soon it was urgent, but he, battering away, seemed ready to stay under forever. She knew she couldn't hold much longer, would have to suck water into her lungs. At the last possible moment he slammed the rock from her hands, pulled her out of the tunnel and, kicking, dragged her up. She kicked madly and burst through the surface gasping for air.

They took new stones and went down again, to work until Kiri again felt her lungs would burst. Then a third time. It seemed hopeless to her, but at last the lock shattered and fell in pieces to the tunnel floor. When Teb pushed the door, it flew open under the pressure of the sea. Again Kiri was frantic for breath. She had a glimpse of the other tunnel opening high in the little cave roof; then they were shooting upward.

She was still sucking in air when Teb dropped back into the sea, too eager to wait. She followed, and found him crouched inside the treasure cave upon a heaped carpet of gold coins, his knees deep in them as he cradled a small, delicate white lyre stained green from the sea light. He raised it to Kiri in salute, his face distorted by the sea; she touched it and felt its power. Then he pushed himself out of the tunnel and they shot upward.

The two dragons nosed the lyre, crooning. It was a beautiful lyre, the ancient ivory delicately carved, the joints perfectly fitted. It held such power that when Teb struck one note the dragons shivered with pleasure.

They carried the ivory lyre up to the crest of the

mountain, to the highest peak so the dragons were in full view of the city. There were battles down in outlying regions, but not many. The dragons' attack had turned the tide; the dark was in retreat.

Standing tall on Seastrider's back, Teb touched one string of the lyre; one note rang out. The rebel soldiers looked up at the mountain, struck still. The lyre's voice was louder, stronger than seemed possible for such a delicate instrument; it filled the city streets and the palace. Teb's voice joined Seastrider's; all their voices joined. All battles ceased and men stood staring at a past so sharply alive they staggered with its power. They knew the pain of past lives, the wrenching challenges. They knew the triumphs. They knew feelings stronger than their own lives had ever permitted, a world immense with possibilities. The dull sickness of the drugs and taverns fell away. Dacia saw its tormentors clearly now for the first time. It understood them, those who sucked on lust and degradation and on terror. The dragon song and the music of the lyre exploded with life into a thousand facets of purpose and strength these peoples had never imagined.

In the black palace, servants ripped off the green tunics that marked their loyalty to the king. Palace guards came awake from their servitude and pulled off their uniforms but did not lay down their swords. Together they marched to the gates to join the gathering townsmen. Then all turned back into the palace, first to the great hall, then, finding it empty, to the king's private quarters.

The dark general and his captains were there with the king. They saw the faces of the townsmen and paled. Those would be the last faces they would see.

When the dark leaders were dead, the people of Dacia marched down into the city to join the troops there, to rid Dacia of other dark captains. But not all men cleaved to the dragon song. For those whose minds had been destroyed, or who preferred evil, there was only dim confusion. They did not see the living past, but only a gray, moving haze. They did not hear the dragon song, but only a few far-off notes that they could not identify. For them, rescue came too late.

As the lyre stilled, as dragon song stilled, the city turned to the mopping up that comes after battle. It was then that a lone man began to climb the black mountain, his mind still filled with the music of lyre and dragons.

He climbed in silence while his troops secured their boat, for they had just crossed the sea from Igness. When he came up over the top of the cliff, black Starpounder keened, then bugled and reared up over the lone figure. Colewolf raised a hand to him, then leaped to his back, and Starpounder rose skyward.

Kiri watched them, choked with joy. She looked at Teb and swallowed back tears. Starpounder circled the mountain bugling as if his strident voice was plenty to speak for both of them, bard and dragon.

Much later, when the dragons and their bards filled the sky, Gram rode behind Kiri, excited as a child. They circled Dacia, swept over Edain and Bukla and the small islands of the archipelago, then dropped down to the sea cliffs that guarded the gate of Gardel-Cloor. The moment the dragons settled, the gate flung open and a little boy ran out, limping hardly at all, and climbed the cliff to them. Teb reached down from Seastrider's back and pulled Marshy up before him, tucking the child's legs into the white harness, and Seastrider swept aloft.

Out over the sea, Marshy sang alone, his voice given power by the dragons and by the bards who, in silence, joined him. Marshy touched each child in the war-ravaged city, made each know special things. He brought the last of the children out of hiding, many who knew nothing but darkness. They came running now, the child-slaves dragging their chains, swarming into Gardel-Cloor, following for the first time not cruel masters but a far greater power.

21

The minute he was on the ground Teb grabbed Camery and squeezed her so hard she yelped. Then he held her away, and they really looked at each other for the first time. She was as tall as he. Her face was smeared with dirt and her bright hair tangled, but her grin was the same, that green-eyed devilish smile. The little girl was still there beneath the strength of a woman and soldier, and the awakened power of a bard. She looked him over and touched the scar on his arm.

"What did that? The scar has twisted your birth-mark—the dragon's mark."

"Sivich's soldiers cut me when they took me captive."

"Garit helped you escape from them, he told me."

"They caught me again outside a fox den at the back of Nison-Serth."

"Then how did you get away?"

"The dragons' mother released me from the dragon

trap Sivich built to catch her. I was the bait. The otters found me with a broken leg and unconscious, and dragged me onto a raft and took me to Nightpool."

She touched his face where a scar marked his chin. "And that? I want to know everything that has happened to you."

He grinned. "I was climbing the sea cliff. A wave made me slip—the sea hydrus was chasing me."

Her eyes widened. She looked down the sea cliff where they stood, at the crashing waves. "So much to learn about you, Teb. So much to tell each other."

Above them on the cliff the dragons had settled among the rocks, twined around one another. The gate of Gardel-Cloor stood ajar. They could hear the tangle of voices inside and the laughter of children who had not laughed for a very long time.

"Camery, I think Mama is alive."

Her eyes widened, not in surprise but in recognition. "I have believed that for a long time. I thought I only wanted to believe it. Tell me . . ."

"She is a bard, did you guess that? She went to search for her own dragon—her second, for the one she paired with originally was killed."

"Where is she?"

"Do you know the Castle of Doors?"

"Oh . . . yes." Camery swallowed, and pressed her fist to her mouth. "She went . . . through? Into . . ."

"Into other worlds. She went searching for Dawncloud, but Dawncloud was here all the time, was fast asleep in Tendreth Slew, so they didn't sense each other. It was Dawncloud who saved me, who is mother of our four."

"But where is Dawncloud now?"

"She went after Mama. But it's a long story; let's save some for later. Garit is down there. I caught a glimpse of him."

They went along the cliff, then down and across stones wet with sea spray, and in through the carved stone gates of Gardel-Cloor. Garit grabbed Teb in a great hug, nearly crushing him, and Camery swept up little Marshy, who ran shouting to her, and whirled him around the great cave, in and out among the shouting children. Teb was surprised to find himself as tall as Garit; Garit had always seemed as huge as the red-maned bull that gave him his nickname. He smelled of horses and leather, and his smile was just as comforting as always. He pummeled Teb and shook him.

"So our Kiri was right. Prince Tebmund of Thedria *was* to be trusted, in spite of consorting with the king."

"Did she say that?"

"She knew she shouldn't trust you so soon, in spite of her feelings. Your strange, perceptive horses upset her."

They looked toward Kiri and Colewolf sitting quietly together, her head on his shoulder and his arm around her. They might have been quite alone, even though dozens of children crowded the cave and bands of rebel fighters kept arriving.

Men and women had begun to remove the children's chains and tend their wounds, and a bathing tub of seawater was heating over a fire, the smoke rising up through a smoke hole. At the back of the fire several haunches were roasting, the smell of crisp meat filling Gardel-Cloor. The great cats wandered among the children, some licking wounds and some curled down among the napping little ones, couching small heads and warming their thin little bodies. And there were foxes. Teb stood staring. Five pale foxes gathered with the great cats, and one old otter.

"Yes, foxes." Garit laughed. "And does the otter make you feel at home? The big fox is Hexet of Kipa. Go and greet them while I help tend to the children; then we'll catch up, have a good talk. I have a thousand questions."

Teb went to sit on a low stone before the animals; he wanted to gather them all in a big hug but wouldn't embarrass them. Just to see foxes again and to see the dark, laughing face of an otter was wonderful. It was only a moment until they were all introduced, and Hexet was telling him that Brux, of the fox colony at Nison-Serth, was his cousin. Brux had helped to save Teb when he escaped the first time from Sivich. And the old otter, Lebekk, knew many at Nightpool, for he had traveled five times to that island.

"I know Thakkur well, and know what he has done for the resistance. Ever since you left Nightpool, Tebriel, he has sent cadres of young armed and trained otters up the coast to help the human rebels in any way they could. At Baylentha, when Ebis the Black put down a second uprising, it was the otters, working in team with Ebis's agents, who discovered the source of the infiltrators and trapped them in their own fishing boats and sank them."

Teb felt a surge of pride in Thakkur so strong he had to swallow several times and could not speak. Thakkur had done it, had made the Nightpool otters into an effective army. He had trained the otters for battle, had taught them to use weapons—despite the loud complaining by Nightpool's handful of trouble-makers.

"And it was Thakkur's otters at Vouchen Vek," Hexet said, "who trained the otter colony there and helped them steal weapons. You were one of them, Lebekk. You were there."

"Yes," Lebekk said, his dark, sleek coat catching the firelight. "With the human rebels, we laid siege to Fekthen and Thiondor, sank their supply boats, and starved the dark troops. We fed the captives secretly and freed them, and they killed their dark masters. Though I think they had other incentives as well. I believe the dragon song touched them there, that visions came to them."

Teb stayed with Lebekk and the foxes a long time, taking pleasure in their eager talk and simple well-being. Then when two great cats challenged them to a game, he left them. The meat was nearly cooked, the cave redolent of the smoky juices, and his stomach rumbled with hunger. He saw more soldiers arriving bloody and torn, having tended first to their tired horses. Now their own wounds were treated and they were fed and made comfortable. Teb found Camery, and they filled their plates with the good roasted meat and roots and flat bread, then found a little alcove where they could sit alone. Here he told her all that had happened to him, from the morning he was led away from the palace tied on his horse. Garit had told her part of it, how he and young Lervey and the old cook, Pakkna, and Hibben of the twisted hand had slipped out of Sivich's camp at midnight, stealing Teb away.

"Pakkna and Lervey are with the troops in Branthen," she said. "Hibben travels across Akemada secretly rallying troops. But tell me again how Sivich captured you."

"As the foxes helped me escape Nison-Serth out a small back entrance, the winged jackals discovered us and attacked. Then Sivich's soldiers were on us. They threw me across a horse—I think that's when my ribs were broken—then rode all night for Baylentha. There they put me in a huge cage made of whole felled trees and barge chain, meaning to capture Dawncloud." He smiled. "But it was Dawncloud who freed me."

He told her how, after four years in the otter colony, he had gone to search for the black hydrus, knowing he must kill it, or it would destroy him. It had captured him and taken him to the drowned city across the open sea. It tried to twist his mind so he would use his bard powers for the dark. "It meant for me to force Seastrider to do the same. But I stabbed it at last, and then the dragons came and finished it.

"All the rooms above water in that place were filled

only with barnacles and sea moss. But there was one apartment in a tall tower that had furnishings—a bed, a chair, clothes, Mama's red dress, and her diary. Merlther Brish's sailboat was tied below waiting for her. But it was her diary that led Dawncloud there and, because she sensed what was in it, led her to the Castle of Doors."

"And you saw Dawncloud go through," she said, studying his face, "into . . . who knows what kind of world. And Mama is there . . . somewhere."

He took her hand. "She will come back. They both will. Now tell me how Garit rescued you. I know he took you to the house of the brewer, where you left your diary for me to find."

She told him the details of her escape, and how she and Garit came to Dacia to the underground, then about her years as servant in the house of Vurbane. Teb could tell she left much unsaid.

"They weren't pleasant years. I didn't think at first I could do such a thing, spy as a servant, be obedient to that dark household. Vurbane is—" She shook her head, her eyes filled with pain. "But I found I could do it. And if I was miserable in some ways, I felt strong inside and . . . well, smug, maybe," she said, laughing, "when I got the information out." She smiled and shook her head. "You won't guess what creature helped me, came to the palace at night to take my messages."

"An owl," he said, laughing. "Was it Red Unat?"

She stared at him. "How did you know his name? Yes, old cranky Red Unat. How . . . ?"

"He came to Nightpool. I asked him to search for you. He went to the tower, then to the house of the brewer. But you had already gone. He brought me your diary. But if he was helping you in Ekthuma, why didn't he tell you about me? Or bring the news to me that you were safe? He knew your name, he . . . Well," Teb said, "but he had never seen you. Still . . ."

"I was called Summer, there. He had no reason to connect me with you. Oh, if he had, if we'd found each other sooner . . ."

"Yes. Well, but it turned out all right."

"It was Red Unat who warned me when Vurbane's troops came to the marketplace to arrest me."

"Yes. I took supper with Vurbane and the dark leaders in Sardira's palace. Vurbane spoke of a great owl, and I guessed it might be Red Unat." Teb took her hand. "I don't like to think about your years with Vurbane. He is . . ."

"Yes. But it's over." She looked at him squarely. "Vurbane is dead." Her words said all that was needed. They looked at each other, each seeing something of the person the other had become.

When they left their private corner, they joined the others, gathered to tell tales of personal victories and defeats that brought them all closer. Everyone had a tale, and evening came on with the entire company still lost in stories. But it was the last tale that filled the bards with excitement. It was this bard vision that would map their days to come and could mean the

245

beginning of final victory over the dark invaders.

Teb had stood the Ivory Lyre of Bayzun on a stone shelf high enough for all to see, the glancing light from the waves through the open gate playing over it. When Colewolf rose from where he sat among the bards, all voices hushed. He went to the lyre and laid his hand on it. No one stirred. As he stood looking at the gathered crowd of humans and animals, a tale began to spin out in silence, making pictures as the dragon song had done. The power of the lyre gave him the power of vision, where for so long he had been mute.

He told a tale of other dragons, of a clutch of new, young dragons somewhere across the western sea.

The tale had been told to Colewolf by a rebel recruit out of Birrig. He had come recently across the vast ocean from the other side of Tirror. There he had sailed beside a tall island peak and stared up to see a dragon lair. He had tied his boat and climbed, to find a lair made of heavy oak trees, with the remains of freshly killed sheep and a shark, and the shells of dragon eggs still caught among the logs.

Teb saw Kiri's eyes alight with excitement, saw Marshy's face transformed, and knew that the same dream gripped them both. Maybe their dragonmates were among the newly hatched clutch. He caught Camery's glance and saw her nod, saw the eager look between Colewolf and Kiri, felt the sense of excitement that gripped the four dragons on the cliff above. They would go there, to the coast of frozen Yoorthed.

That night Teb tried to sleep in a small cave off the large one and could not. He rose at last and left the caves, to find Seastrider sleeping soundly, dreaming, stretched out between boulders. She woke and moved around to make a place for him, and he settled down with his back against her, the sea wind cool in his face. He was just dozing off when he saw Camery come up, silhouetted against the thin moonlight, and go to settle down beside Nightraider. The big dragon blew a warm breath against her back with a huffing sound. Teb heard Camery sigh as if very contented.

"Colewolf sleeps beside Starpounder," Seastrider told him. "And Kiri and Marshy are curled together, there, between Windcaller's forefeet. We are all here, Tebriel. Rest now, for soon we search for dragons—baby dragons."

"Yes. And for Quazelzeg, on the dark continent."

"Do you remember once, Tebriel, you told me of predictions that the white otter of Nightpool made, the night before you left there?"

"That I would ride the winds of Tirror. We've done that, all right. That I would . . . travel to mountains far to the north, and go among wonderful creatures there."

"And what else?"

"That I would know pain. That there was a street in Sharden's city narrow and mean, that there is danger there, and it reeks of pain. Thakkur had said, 'Take care, Tebriel, when you journey into Sharden.' "

"Sharden lies at the center of the dark continent, Tebriel. But I am with you now. We are all together now."

He slept at last, restlessly, dreaming not of the dark continent but of baby dragons, of a cadre of dragons and bards so large and powerful it could drown the dark with its song. He woke at first light to see Kiri standing out on the edge of the cliff staring down at the sea. He went out to her. They stood watching as the four dragons fished far out over the waves, diving with folded wings, then leaping into the sky carrying shark that, this morning, they ate on the wing, their spirits too high even to come ashore. He saw the yearning in Kiri's face, for a dragon to whom to belong.

"If there is another clutch of dragons," he said, "your mate could be among them."

"But how long will it take to find them? I won't be with you, I won't know . . ."

"Of course you'll be with us."

"But—"

"Do you think we'd leave a bard behind? Do you think your father would leave you?"

"It's his job, to be where he's needed."

"Not without you, not anymore. It's your job to be with us."

She didn't say anything. After a while he turned her chin to him and saw her tears. He wiped them from her cheeks. She looked at him, so deep into his eyes. Then she smiled. They turned together to stare out at the sea. The dragons were returning, sweeping so low to the water that their wind beat the sea into waves.

"We will need harness," he said.

"There is soft leather among the supplies." She licked a last tear from her upper lip and turned to race down the cliff.

He found Camery and they went down into the caves to prepare for their journey. He hated good-byes. He wished he would not soon have to say them, that there never had to be a good-bye.

Garit said, "We will move into the castle, Tebriel. We will open the windows and whitewash the walls, take down all that velvet. It can be our garrison, a meeting place for a new Dacian council, a fine stable for young riders, room enough for every child who cares to come. And a room for you, Tebriel, kept for your use alone."

"Then I have two rooms of my own to come back to, for there is my cave at Nightpool. One day there'll be a third, when we win back the Palace of Auric."

"When you win back the Palace of Auric . . . I would like to be with you on that mission."

"Then so you shall," he said, and could imagine that palace whole again, clean, filled with color and sunlight, with his mother there and with dragons in Auric's skies and on the meadows.

It took two days to make harness, sharpen weapons, and prepare themselves. On the morning of the third day they were ready, and all along the shore above Gardel-Cloor and in the city streets folk gathered, cheering as the dragons leaped skyward.

They banked on the wind. The shadows of their wings washed across upturned faces. The war in Dacia was finished, the un-men gone from this island continent. It was time to touch other shores where the dark still ruled. Seastrider climbed straight up with powerful wings. Teb touched the strings of the lyre. Its voice rang out alone, powerful and true. Nothing was impossible; all dreams could be made real if they strove fiercely enough. Seastrider lifted fast into cloud, and Teb saw Kiri and Marshy laughing up at him from between Windcaller's pale wings. Then the two black dragons sped by him racing, Camery and Colewolf leaning flat to their necks.

High above cloud, the dragons settled to a steady pace and headed northwest toward the wide sea and unfamiliar lands, to search for new young dragons.